OCTAVIAN TALES

OCTAVIAN TALES

Brad Shprintz

Contents

For Brenda Crosby and John Karnehm - your kindness
carried me farther than you know, and reminded me
that real goodness still exists in this world.

1

THE MEETING

The rain was pounding against the windowpane, from soft to hard as the waves of water banged against it. This was no weather manipulation but rather Mother Nature's true vitality revealed.

"Study windows opaque," commanded Scott Howard, who was tired of seeing the water bouncing, yet did enjoy the noise it generated. His thoughts were on the meeting he just had with the greatest man of the twenty-second century. Replaying it in his memory, making sure he had not missed any subtle gestures.

It felt surreal having a meeting with the great Lord John Husk, the most brilliant, self made, charismatic, eloquent man, some considered him a genius. His rise to power began with inventions, yet his greatest talent was building an empire.

Society had separated into three classes, the lowest being the general population. Known by the other classes as leeches, they produced nothing just constantly consuming to fill the time. Eating, watching holograms, playing simulation games, which felt quite real and sleeping. A few played physical sports.

The general population were allowed relationships but having children were strictly controlled. If allowed, only one for each couple. Children were raised by the cities left on Earth, having periodic visits back with their families.

The middle class was quite small consisting of specialized people with talents needed by the machines also known as AIE, Alien Intelligence Entities and the Lords. This middle-group consisting of scientists, highly skilled artisans, and others with a potpourri of skills. To the Lords they were tools.

Lords owned and ruled all things within their cities and worlds, that included money, businesses, judgments, plus many personal options for what the leeches and tools could have.

Scott Howard was average in weight and height, sporting a thin haircut and serious attitude. Being soft spoken while still having a powerful presence, he was a researcher; in the past his title would had been a reporter. Sure, computers can read everything within the spectrum of electronics and even physical books. Finding esoteric data involves more than that, at his early age he had already created a reputation for finding deep hidden knowledge.

Scott lived in one of the many cities, where all the leeches resided. It was in a nice section and considered the high end for what it was. Travel within the cities were not too restrictive, compared to traveling to another city or off planet. Those were strongly controlled by the Lords.

The rain was getting stronger, the heavy waves of water with their sounds getting closer together. A reminder of humanity's limits, Scott thoughts went to Lord John Husk.

He made his appearance with a breakthrough in physics thought to be law. Entropy being his target. Bringing him a great fortune, for most that would have been enough, not John Husk.

He turned his talents to the financial betting arena; the stock markets which were still around now with Planets and Lords values also traded. John's talents there were as amazing as his other accomplishments. A nice fortune turned into incredible wealth. Again, most would relax and enjoy all those successes.

Besides all that, he was blessed with being a great orator, his speeches on many different subjects were not just memorable but educational. When looking up the definition of having everything a person could want, there was Lord John Husk's name and picture.

Scott had been transported to one of his personal planets, extraordinary is just a word. His home had hundreds of servants; perched over a cliff while also stretching in all other directions. Motorized walkways transported the important people plus John's family, the rest moved as quickly as they could, the structure being immense in trying to get around.

Rooms were the sizes of regular homes that sat inside the structure. There were too many kitchens, bathrooms, bedrooms, and specialty areas to count.

Scott was brought into an office the likes of which he could never imagine. One wall made of glass had a jungle on the other side. They must have been well fed as many diverse types of animals were there, from predators to their victims. All just enjoying the sun together.

As he waited to meet the man everyone knew, yet so few had ever met, wondering what he was doing here. John was a prompt man, with Scott not waiting long for their first meeting to begin.

"Mr. Scott Howard, thank you for your visit, I hope all was to your liking?"

John finished that with an outstretched hand and smile, it had taken Scott by surprise. He did not expect him to be prompt let alone polite, this making his response a bit slower.

"It is an honor to meet you Lord Husk, I have never seen a home such as yours, its magnificence is overwhelming."

"Please call me John or anything you like just not Lord; you are a guest in my home. I want you to contact a certain individual and get him here." At that he stopped, looking hard at Scott, evaluating if he had made the right choice.

"I have his information plus a pocket watch I am sure he will want returned to him. Your part is described in detail within these papers." Handing him a folder plus a small square box.

Scott's first thoughts were why me, of course Lord Husk did not want to do it himself. Lords only do what they want, actions they enjoy. Trying to get someone over for dinner is not their style, but why choose him?

John was perceptive and answered his question before asked, that is, even if Scott would have mentioned it.

"You are curious why I have chosen you for this task. I viewed your post on that man in the paperwork, I also want you to start the most detailed review of his life from as far back as it goes, he is full of surprises. Now when you complete this project successfully you will receive an upgrade in living conditions plus a sizable number of credits. Well, what do you say?"

"Of course I accept, I will do my best, yes, he was highly active twenty years ago, they said the best historian of the nineteenth, twentieth, and twenty-first centuries. Then he completely disappeared." As he finished, he looked at the paperwork that had one name at the top, Octavian Blanche Wright.

Scott was still sitting in his apartment; the rain had died down with the waves ceasing and just a steady downpour as its replacement. His thoughts were about geniuses and how to him they fall into two categories.

One group can focus extremely deep in one area, getting to levels others never thought. Seeing the problem from every perspective to the smallest minuscule detail. With that talent plus being incredibly smart, they create something new or so greatly improved that a genius could only do it. Nikola Tesla and his incredible knowledge of electricity with all its ramifications and Albert Einstein with his mathematical formulas and gravitational theories are examples of that group.

Then there is the type that make a difference in so many areas, their gift spread out affecting a multitude of sciences. Sir Isaac Newton was an example, from math to astronomy, alchemy, and biblical studies, not to mention optics of light. His laws of motion became a bedrock of physics.

Lord John Husk reminded Scott of Sir Isaac Newton; his reach touched many areas of life.

Scott's thoughts went to the article he posted about Octavian. He had framed it from the Lord's perspective and decided to review it, even before he went thru the paperwork sitting in front of him.

It was his last lecture about the prior three centuries yet this time he did not follow his usual presentation. After visiting seven cities that were owned by various Lords, that was his final show. There were strict rules regarding all presentations, recordings of any type were never allowed. Yet this time someone had made an audio recording which was then transcribed and became viral. That moment did not last long while at the same time, Octavian disappeared from the public eye.

Most assumed he was transferred to an educational center for what he had said. The Lords always acted like they wanted free speech unless it was derogatory to them or their agendas.

After contacting various people who had attended that lecture and getting information that was not written down, he had a better idea of the fiasco.

Scott read the transcript aloud, wishing he would have heard the real interchange. There is so much to be learned about tones and cadence, and the pausing between words. Even hand or body movements can make a significant difference in interpretations. He would have to make do with what he had, that being a common factor of current life.

Octavian: "Personal freedom had decreased each century, during the nineteenth and twentieth centuries, there would have been a revolution by the people if told where they could travel, of course there were repressive countries but nothing like the restrictions of today."

Scott thinking that was when the crowd started to turn on him, yet he was smiling, enjoying their anger. If anything, it pushed Octavian more to rile the audience.

A woman from the leeches shouted: "We were free to come and see you!"

Octavian: "Actually I came to see you, if I did not speak in this city, you would not be allowed to travel to other cities to see me. I am free and can travel where I please, you are limited to one city, so who is seeing who."

Scott thinking the crowd was booing him and shouting profanities, only making Octavian laugh and continue.

Octavian: "Now the people making the loudest noise are lost and there is no hope for them, look around you and if you see someone who looks like they are thinking, follow them, they may see the light, there may be time for them."

The crowd was screaming and throwing items onto the stage as he continued.

Octavian: "You do realize that your craniums are getting smaller, that is because your brains are shrinking and there is less need for the prior size. And that is not the worse part of it..."

At that point, his mic was turned off, maybe because he might have been attacked by the leeches, or the Lords made it happen, which ever the case, he was whisked away. They said he was smiling and laughing during the entire incident. From that point on Octavian was never mentioned and just faded from the news.

Scott now thinking about it, how did he get permission from the three Lords, Husk being one of them to travel and do the shows. It was standard procedure to arrange events to keep the leeches entertained. All his other lectures were of the standard type, yet this last one he wanted to make a statement.

Scott had written a post of how ungrateful Octavian was and wrong about his comments. Showing examples of certain special people being able to travel beyond the city. They were the rare exceptions, yet the leeches ate it up. Anything to reinforce their beliefs were gold to them.

The folder in front of him sat with the small package, Scott decided to go thru the papers inside the folder and then the watch within the package.

The information went over all that was known about Octavian Blanche Wright, his history seemed fabricated to Scott. There was a note to check other names associated with Octavian. That list was long, making it feel like he must have been doing many illegal actions, forcing all those name changes.

They were numbered but not in any particular order, all pointing back to the description and some even with pictures of Octavian.

These all cannot be right, were Scott's thoughts, some were in the twenty-first century, others were in the twentieth century. He figured it would be easy to debunk the earliest names and then work backwards. These types of mysteries were right up his alley.

He continued reading the report, it said his primary goal was to get Octavian to Lord Husk's home on planet Husk. Currently Octavian was on the planet LaTaFree. He would be provided with transfer passes and credits to get there while using the watch as a bargaining chip to get Octavian back to Lord Husk.

It is imperative that he travel with Octavian and not rely on his promise to come. The report ended reiterating that the mission will only be considered a success when both returned to Husk's planet.

—-

There are few places within the galaxy that compare to LaTaFree, the greatest entertainment giant that had ever been created. Something for everyone, were one of its motto, they had many different slogans. There were mountains to climb, water ways to conquer, plays, parks, sports for participation or just to watch.

Museums, musical presentations, learning centers covering many different studies, the list of their activities seem to be unending. It was the galaxy's vacation resort, truly being unique among so many planets.

LaTaFree had many visitors, thousands of varied species all coexisting together. This was not just by luck or everyone's good intentions. They had one of the best security forces any planet could want. It is the last place to start or have trouble in.

One of the greatest aspects of living life there was its stability. Their form of government transitions was not by chance, which led to very consistent laws and procedures. The bottom line it was one of the safest, most enjoyable places to be within the galaxy.

Most could not afford to visit, those that could, only stayed a brief time. Leaving the locals and the incredibly lucky few foreigners who had permission to live there permanently. It was extremely expensive yet wonderful to be part of a community like that.

Octavian enjoyed the bench by the lake, there was a park adjacent to it having a section of toys, swings, and other amusements for the children. He liked watching them, sometimes telling stories, mostly just spending time around young people. He had moved off the bench and was laying on the lawn playing an injured soldier.

The three boys and two girls were gang tackling him as he cried out, "I surrender!"

There were two adults watching Octavian, they were not human but close in form and DNA. They had an Asian type of appearance. It was a small community where everyone really watched out for each other. That with an incredible security force brought a peaceful fantasy feeling of serenity.

Once Octavian was back home, his family which included the two watching him plus their two children. They were not really family but treated him as their father with the upmost respect. His wishes to them were commands and his survival the most paramount aspects of their lives.

He liked his routines and would stick quite strictly in keeping them. Now it was off to eat and then read, after that some snacks then writing, as he was very fond of doing. Plus, some walks around LaTaFree, Octavian loved to study all types of beings.

The roadways were curved and then straightened out to show huge circles, inside the circles were live music events or sometimes plays acted out in all their glory. Around the four points of the circle, north, east, south, and west, had people selling food, clothing, souvenirs, and things of that nature.

Each major circles were like parties and circuses combined. There were so many diverse creatures all getting along fine. Living their lives as they pleased with the golden rule, hurt no one and no one will hurt you.

—-

Lord Husk unlike most great men knew when a sharp tongue or gentle word were needed and applied them accordingly. As eloquent as he were at times, he could be brutally short and severe. Like others with great power, they are always feared and envied by all except when around equals. There just were so few equals.

At age fifty-two he became obsessed with his short life. He had applied so much energy in his youth, figuring out all sort of things and rewarded well for it. Time, he now realized was the true enemy. Regular life still only lasted to one hundred and ten years at best, with the last ten to fifteen not very pretty. In his mind, someone as great as he, deserved much more time than that.

There were clones but they were still not reliable, The AIE also had a solution, but one's humanity would be lost living in an android. He wanted to extend his current existence staying within the body he now lived in.

He already knew Octavian secret about his extended life. Yet knowing something was different from being able to replicate it. He had spent a small fortune on several ways, all failed or could not get past certain points with their development.

Once Octavian was within his home, he would have that secret or Octavian Blanche Wright would die.

Scott had sent a message to the address given in the paperwork, even if the message was not read or sent back with a negative outcome, he would make the trip.

First, he realized this was more than just trying to get someone to visit Lord Husk. If he failed, it would be the end for him. At best he would lose all his rankings, having to start at the bottom regarding living, eating, and any enjoyment he would look for.

Second, even if he received a negative response, he might be able to per-swayed Octavian in person.

Third, he had never been to an open world. Yes, he had been off Earth, but only to the Lords owned worlds.

The reports conveyed death and destruction waiting for anyone not under the Lord's protection. That they were blessed not to have that type of chaos upon them.

Sadly, he had not heard back from Octavian; after waiting two weeks, he really wanted a positive response, decided it was time for his visit. Even with the importance of this assignment and thoughts of potential failure, the excitement of his first visit to an uncontrolled world was overwhelming.

Scott packed light having only one bag that also worked as a backpack. There was the transfer center, which everyone used even when traveling from one city to another. A separate building with a long hallway connected to the transfer center. That building used for off world travel.

Even with his proper paperwork, plus a signed letter by Lord Husk himself, Scott was checked and rechecked three times as he waited for the craft's departure. Twice the three men had made calls while doing their checks.

Both buildings were exceptionally large and beautifully decorated, their size only accentuated the lack of people within them. There were more security personnel than travelers. Scott's thoughts went to what if he never went back, could his chip implant be manipulated from that distance? It was just a passing thought with the next being how would he survive? The fear of the unknown may be the greatest chains that hold people in the same spot. While Scott waited, he pulled out his favorite book, The Art of War by Sun Tzu. He had read it many times, with each re-reading gaining new insights.

Finally, he boarded the ship, which was small, assigned a private room and informed they would arrive in two days. Meals would be served in the dining room between the times listed. The room did have a hologram, and small water room. They made two more pick-ups before they began the journey.

There was a group lounge opened to all the passengers onboard. On the second day a few hours before his arrival there was a passenger, non-human, he had been talking with. When Scott asked if he had ever been to Earth, the response surprised him.

"Oh, not recently, last time was about one-hundred and fifty years ago. Hear it has changed greatly since then and have no present or future plans to return."

Then realizing that his comment sounded bad, added "I am sure it is quite lovely, just been very busy lately."

Scott thinking, they were told there were long lines of people wanting to visit Earth, that they were lucky to be able to live there. Instead of fearing the unknown that was coming, it felt more like a relief leaving where he had been.

People around him were more relaxed than Earthlings, that feelings spread to his current spirit. Feeling positive about his future outcome, even without a reply or invite. He realized how much the environment around him played with his emotions. There was a negativity on Earth that just was not present on the ship.

Not sure what he expected, all that can be said is it was so much greater than whatever those expectations were. The size of the welcome center at LaTaFree was gigantic, even more impressive was how many different life forms were there. Between the quantity and variety of beings, Scott felt overwhelmed.

He heard of such things but really seeing it can not be described but only experienced. Also, everyone was genuinely nice to each other, his mind reasoning that they were all on vacation. It was so different than how they had been told, expecting everyone to be holding their guns, ready to shoot within an instant.

Another aspect that surprised Scott was how many people had jobs, simple jobs like taking transfer passes or answering questions. All that had been relegated to machines on Earth, with truly little human work done or required.

The hosts as they called themselves seemed to be happy, enjoying the tasks at hand. The lines moved quickly and now it was his turn. She was not human but very pleasant to look at. After going thru his paperwork plus electronic passes, she looked into his eyes and said the following.

"Mr. Howard, you are traveling to a restricted area so you will need to use this special pass to get in there. I hope you will enjoy your stay and please contact this person,"

She pointed to a picture with a name and contact information, "For any special requests or just help in finding the perfect attractions that suits your interests."

With a big smile and giving him some items he went past the next set of doors. They led to the first of many circles that LaTaFree had. That day was a musical play which greeted new visitors. It was amazing to watch and hear, with many waiting around that first circle.

Scott feeling a sense of urgency saw some official looking people and asked for help in getting to Octavian's home. They were very friendly with one of them walking him to the development.

After walking two blocks that were curved, they came upon what looked like an old road, not used. Once walking it for about half a mile the park and tourist feeling were gone, what lay in front of them was a wide-open area. There was a crater structure with grass and some trees rising to a height of fifty feet ending with it open to the sky.

A path led to a security checkpoint. After Scott's pass was shown and the two officials spoke with each other, his prior guard left leaving the new guard that provided details on how to get to Octavian's home.

"One is located on the left with the house up the hill, it has a tower on it, hard to miss."

His directions were easy to follow and within a brief time, Scott was at Octavian's front door.

He knocked and waited but there was no response, while also looking for a bell or electronic device to make his presence known. Finding nothing of that sort, he sat on a bench that was near the door.

Taking more time to observe his surroundings, it had a unique layout. There were many gentle hills with curving walkways leading to the dwellings. The homes were half above and half below the hills they sat on. From the surface they all had a small similar appearance yet when entered they felt and were bigger than they looked.

After a half hour Scott knocked on the door again with this time an Asian looking woman appeared, giving him a dirty look and spoke.

"Go away!"

Scott was both elated to finally have contacted someone yet also distressed about her message and attitude.

"I do apologize for showing up unexpectedly, I have important business for Mr. Wright and a gift I know he will want, please allow me entrance and an audience." After saying that Scott put on his best smile which was not natural for him.

She looked somewhere under thirty but above twenty-five, giving him a hard long look and then squinting her eyes, responded. "Go away!" With that she slammed the slightly open door.

He sat back down on the bench, his spirits crushed, what could he do? Going back home without even getting a meeting would look awful. As his mind pondered on his future actions, a thought came. I will just sit here, eventually he will leave or come home, what other options are there, he was deep in thought when the children inter-rupted.

"Are you waiting to play with One?" A young boy asked.

"Well, I am waiting for Mr. Wright." Scott replied, then seeing their confusion added.

"Mr. Octavian Blanche Wright," hoping that would clear the matter up.

The boy then said, "Well we want to play with One." With that he went to the door and knocked. Within a moment the door opened, the woman who had just spoken to Scott was so sweet when she explained that One unfortunately could not play today but promised he would tomorrow. That pacified the gang of youngsters who then moved on to the playground.

By the time Scott had looked back at the door, it was shut. Feeling defeated but resolved he would wait it out. The problem with that type of feeling is as time goes bye the strength in the resolve fades likes sands in an hourglass. It had now been three hours of waiting, he was hungry, tired, and feeling abused by everyone, Lord Husk, Octavian, and especially the young lady of the home.

Knocking now harder than before, expecting the woman's anger, the door opened with an old man sitting in an old wheelchair, and said the following.

"Your mad at having to wait three hours, yes?"

The frankness of the statement just heard, combined with his anger, he wanted to respond with yes.

Scott answered, "No, I appreciate your time, Mr. Wright." Ending again with a smile, thinking he would have to work on smiling.

"Let's get something straight right now, if you don't provide me with complete honesty on all my questions, I will shut this door, call security and you will be removed. So, I am going to ask again and understand I know you did not come here by your own concern. You were sent and feel slighted that I made you wait this long."

"I have come a long way to give you a gift, it felt like a long time but that is my perception and am delighted to speak with you." With that he did not even try to smile.

Octavian was just having fun, so he continued, "Do you know how I know you were sent?"

Scott speaking quickly answered, "No." By this time he was aggravated with Octavian, who he knew was treating him poorly.

Octavian continued, "Let me tell you a story, when I was incredibly young there was a girl, I loved. I drove to her home, uninvited like you!" At that he looked at Scott and smiled.

"I waited five hours for her to come home, eventually her mother invited me inside. Explained she would be away all night, please stop waiting and go home. I would have been happy to wait twice that long to see that girl, because it was what my heart wanted. Of course, if someone sent me, I would never wait that long. And if I did, I would be as mad as you currently are."

Scott then at that moment realized he was dealing with someone who was not as he seemed, he was used to lessor minds most of the time. Octavian was smarter than he looked and realized getting him to go anywhere he did not desire was not going to be easy.

Octavian invited him into his home so they could discuss whatever Scott had on his mind.

The home was bigger inside as there were two large rooms that were completely underground. At the end of one of those rooms was a library office, which obviously Octavian spent much time within. There were two large comfortable chairs, both the same in size and style, with a small stand-alone table between them.

A young man appeared close to the same age as the young lady and moved one of the chairs allowing Octavian's wheelchair its space.

Once he pulled out his pipe, loaded it and began to light the contents within, Octavian spoke.

"Mr. Scott Howard, why are you here and please do not mention my old pocket watch."

Scott had put the small box on the desk between them and answered.

"Lord Husk would like to meet you and has sent me to ask. His home is magnificent and has plenty of space plus anything you might want for your short visit there."

Octavian looked displeased, "Why do you think he has asked me to go?"

Scott usually would lie in a situation like this, give some answer that is plausible without revealing the true nature to such a question. Octavian had bright blue eyes, his brown hair showing frequent shades of gray, his face had lines, some hard. But his eyes still had a young look. It was hard to lie to those eyes, which were focus totally on his own.

"Sir, you are very wise, far smarter than I or most on Earth, maybe it is to have a stimulating conversation with someone like yourself." Scott had never looked away while answering.

The answer was either unacceptable or not what Octavian was looking for. He tried again to get his answer, or maybe it was to probe what Scott really knew.

"Does it have to do with my age?" His blue eyes fixed upon Scott, searching for any movement, something that would be a tell-tale sign that he knew.

"Sir, since you mentioned that subject, I am a researcher and have investigated the history of your life. Do you have a grandfather that resembles you?" Scott ended there, waiting for the most obvious answer that would solve the dilemma.

Octavian replied quickly and with a smile, "No."

Scott decided to use a different approach, "Sir, Mr. Wright, would you mind if I inquired on how old you are."

"Please call me Octavian, no need to be formal here, we are friends, correct? Even the Lords are controlled by time. You know how old I am, especially if you are a researcher. I have had many different names. In that regard, I do not know how anyone can use just one name thru out their existence. We change so much, not just physically but who we really are. Once that happens it is time for a new name to acknowledge the event."

Then he smiled again, bigger but it had sadness within it, "Older than you think."

Scott's first thought was Octavian should have been a politician. Such a long answer that clarified nothing, he wondered if he should press the issue or let it go.

Octavian's attention then went to the watch. He opened the box, inspected the pocket watch, and put it in his pocket. He did not thank Scott or act like it meant anything.

"I imagine life would be better for you if I accompanied you to John Husk's home. Realize my family will not be happy. It will take me three days to get ready, during that time you are a guest here. I recommend that you check out some of what LaTaFree has to offer."

Scott could not believe what his ears just heard. All his prayers had been answered, of course he was surprised how quickly Octavian consented. It all now felt, just to easy, wrong in a way that currently was hard for him to define. Whatever the reasons, it was what he needed.

"Thank you, Mr. Wright, Octavian," after that he was at a lost for words which was unusual for Scott, "I know Lord Husk will be delighted to hear the news."

2

QUEST FOR IMMORTALITY

Each city had its people problems, there always were a few that rebelled against the Lords, AIE, and each other. How it was dealt with, was up to the Lord that owned that city. Illegal broadcast and recordings were a constant problem.

Controlling information was the key to keeping the leeches contained. There was always constant talk of thinning their numbers even more, yet they still had importance. Their money did not matter to the Lords and AIE, but their DNA did. Also, as test subjects on whatever needed testing.

Then there were the rare ones, that had special talents in creativity, researching specific areas, and beauty. Regardless, control must always be enforced. They must never forget who their master was, were the thoughts of John Husk.

John was a large man in height and body type. His bald head was accentuated by his big beard and eyes. His look went deep into the people he dealt with.

The core of all problems was freedom, leeches wanting more in all areas. He remembered one of his old teachers who thoughts were truly clear on that subject.

Never invite the peasants to the banquet, do not even give them the scraps that are left. What they do not know, they will not want, was how his instructor had put it. Then more came to his mind, the fastest way to a revolution is a taste of what was or might be.

The teacher tried to impart that kindness really works in reverse. He related a story of an old peasant that never had eaten meat. One day, the prince feeling kind, gave the man a wonderful meat dish. Afterwards he asked the peasant how he felt, the answer was very insightful.

The peasant said it was the best and worst day of his life. Wonderful was the taste of the cooked meat yet also terrible that he had never had it prior or will have it again. That, his teacher said was the problem with kindness.

The real trick is applying just the right amount of pressure to make others not want that treatment without making the perpetrators martyrs. If done correctly the former negative action can turn into a current positive result. John was playing out different scenarios, evaluating which would be the best to do.

He received the message that Scott would be returning with Octavian Wright. John was quite pleased with that, also in his choosing Scott to get it done. John was as honest as he could be to himself, he had doubts whether Scott could succeed.

His dreams of extended life, which he had many people working on in separate ways to achieve that, all had failed, this felt different. Feeling incredibly positive that it would happen, he chose the softer plan of punishment for the rebel leeches.

John wondered what his first meeting with Octavian would be like. The man that led the Final Battle, most knew nothing about that, it had happened over one hundred years ago. Yet there was so much more, usually with death and destruction following him.

That was one of the reasons he persuaded the other Lords to let Octavian do his presentations. They knew nothing of his past, John wanted to observe him closer. Octavian was unique in the chip given to him from the First People. Just studying that would be worth so much in knowledge.

When you have everything, it is rare to be excited. Now thinking about the potential to not only have his life extended, possibly forever, yet to also gain access to what is inside Octavian's head.

He had a room setup for his disability, that factor disappointed him. The thought of being impaired for an extended period never entered into his mind. John's current focus had been on politics.

Even with just a little over ten Lords, there were always issues between them. Some were on the rise while others and their cities declining. It was fertile ground for deals. Alliances made and broken, but there were no wars. That had been agreed on. It was one of the reasons the leeches agreed to the present conditions. With the Lord's control the world was safer, that taught to the leeches and repeated to them often.

—-

Life in LaTaFree was amazing to Scott, everything being incredible. So much to do, with all areas open to travel, the freedom that everyone had was a shock to his senses. He would be happy to spend the rest of his life, here in LaTaFree.

His suspicions were that Lord Husk had ill intentions for Octavian. If correct and knowing he had help make that happen, sadden his spirits. Thinking to himself, sure Octavian can be a pain, yet he is incredibly wise. Seeing him play with the children, made Scott think Octavian had some good in him, and leading him to Lord Husk was the wrong action to do.

His family as Octavian called them, were upset about his leaving, especially not taking someone other than Scott with him. They were polite to him, given his guest status, yet that was all he would get.

It was at the beginning of the third day while the man and woman of the home were getting ready for Octavian's departure. The others in the home were children of the young couple and were oblivious of what was taking place.

The woman cornered Scott and said the following, "He has done remarkable things with more to come. It is now your job to protect him with your life; promise me you will do this!"

Her face had not looked away from his, her eyes had an intensity, like they were looking into his soul, seeing if he were worthy and strong enough to complete the task.

She said again, "Repeat my words and promise me with your life that you will not fail."

Scott looked at the woman, wondered if anyone would ever be that concerned for him. His life had no permanent relationships, which had never troubled him. Just her sincere concern for Octavian was priceless.

"I will protect him with my life; I promise you he will return unharmed." Scott responded. Assuming he would not have to risk his life, and that Octavian would be fine. In hindsight that was a foolish assumption.

Leaving LaTaFree was hard for anyone, it is not just all the attractions, the people all were happy. There being such strong positive vibrations that surrounded the homes and everyone. Instead of one transportation center, many different areas had services. It was quite easy to leave and arrive wherever a traveler had chosen.

Octavian was quiet during the trip which only lasted two days and one night of traveling. They went directly to Lord Husk's personal planet; its creation was to make an impression. The fact that Octavian was using an old-fashioned wheelchair, that had no power of its own, made the situation hard. The current handicap devices deployed a minimal anti-gravity unit, making moving up stairs to landings and such quite easy. Not to mention not having to push your way thru the world.

Scott's thoughts were Octavian was full of contradictions. He was extremely educated in many different sciences yet avoided most of the conveniences they provided. His wheelchair was so outdated, he must know there are much better ones available.

The greeting they received was much more intense than Scott's prior visit. Live music plus two rows of people, one on each side of the walkway to the home that greeted them, tossing flowers in front of their path.

Scott thoughts were this would be how victorious warriors returning from battle were greeted. It was elaborate in size, making him feel proud to accomplish his mission. They tried to help Octavian push his wheelchair; the walkway paved with beautiful flat stones. He declined their offers and slowly pushed himself forward, making the process much slower than it needed to be.

He was smiling and enjoyed the show of welcome, when they arrived at the stairs to the extraordinary home, they helped Octavian by picking up his wheelchair and placing him on the landing.

After arriving in Lord John Husk's study, his personal security agent plus oldest daughter, Serenity, were present. Finishing out the assembly was Scott and Octavian, this was a private meeting,

Lord John Husk sat behind his desk, the glass wall separating them from the animals on his left. His daughter was on his right side standing, while his strategic genius, Mr. G, was on the left.

Octavian sat in front of John; a chair was moved so that could be carried out. Scott sat on the chair off to the side on Octavian's right, which at this point was not at all in front of Lord Husk.

With voice commands the glass separating the jungle from John's study became opaque, making the room feel more private. The lights were soft and pleasant, music was playing.

John began with, "Welcome to my home, it is an honor to have your presence, considering how long you have lived and all you have done. Thank you for your visit, I have the best physicians in the Galaxy, if you allow them to help, they might be able to fix your current situation. At least let me give you the latest in technology to aid you in traveling. This is my oldest daughter, Serenity, who also wanted to make your acquaintance."

Then stopped to hear what response he would receive.

Octavian listen politely yet looked amused by the prior statement.

"John, thank you for your offers but I will decline them. I take life as it gives with the good and bad, not trying to mask my handicaps. We both know what you want and that will only happen under my conditions."

Octavian had never taken his eyes off John, both men had strong stares, eyes that penetrated others, but had no effect on either man.

Lord Husk was patient and polite, in control of his emotions and gently said.

"Mr. Wright, this can be pleasant for everyone involved. It is apparent that you have the weaker hand, I will still treat you fairly and make it profitable in some way that will benefit you."

Now Octavian had a big smile, almost laughing and started in a different direction.

"As you know I like history, so before I answer your last statement, I have some questions. Am I correct in assuming you gave Mr. Scott my watch to give to me?"

Without waiting for an answer, he continued, "You had your solution sitting right in the palm of your hand and gave it away. Then Mr. Scott did the same thing." Now Octavian was laughing and continued.

"Let me tell you the history of that watch, it was my Grandmother's Father's watch. She gave it to me, and I eventually gave it to Bubba Jones. I also gave Bubba a Jinn which he put into that watch. Later he gave it to Jayne Stillwater who then used it and gave it back to Bubba. At that point I lost its history, yet you, John Husk found it and gave it to Mr. Scott who gave it back to me. At the time I made no big deal in its re-acquisition. Later that night I wondered if the Jinn was still in there. Like you and Scott no one ever made a wish around it. The Jinn was in that watch, but I could not make another wish. I had already used it once. So, I had a member of my family make the wish for me. It just seems so ironic that all you wanted you already had, just not the knowledge of what it was."

Octavian was obviously trying to get Lord John Husk mad or at least annoyed and it had worked.

"Now to your former statement about my weaker hand, I do not perceive it that way. Please allow me to show you, my reasoning. I am not afraid to die; truth is I can activate my death at any moment with the chip in my head. With my death that chip will also self-destruct. Which leads me to my second point, you have so much, homes, planets, slaves, scientists, all manner of resources yet with all that."

Now he hesitated, driving in the point he was going to make.

"You can not do what I can give you. If you could there would be no need for me. I want nothing from you, am not afraid of you killing me and know you can not torture me. I have the one thing you cannot get, so from my perspective until you get what I have, you have the weaker hand."

John was many things; most might have let their ego override good judgment. He started like Octavian in a different direction.

"What did you have your servant wish for? Where is the Jinn now, just give me that and this business will be concluded."

Octavian who had now taken a serious tone responded, "No one can now get the Jinn, that power is too much for any of us. I was in the room when he made the wish, of course I did not see it. Once the Jinn comes out, time stops and only the recipient can see and hear. My son conveyed that the Jinn asked him if he was sure that was his wish, which it always does. Then he said the Jinn had a smile of relief, like a sentence that had finally been served. Imagine being a servant for eternity. I set the Jinn free with the wish that he would forever be unreachable."

Octavian then changed the subject to a more positive tone.

"I will make the elixir of extended life and go over my terms tomorrow for doing it. Currently I would like to relax and tomorrow if acceptable to you, I will begin. If you could have someone lead me to my room, that would be wonderful."

That statement pleased Lord John Husk, now it was just a case of negotiation with the prize in hand.

John replied, "Of course, after a good night's rest we will go over the terms to our agreement."

Serenity then spoke up, "Father I would be happy to push Mr. Wright to his suite, if that is acceptable to you."

John thinking his daughter was just like himself, Octavian was an interesting person.

"Of course, my dear." Said with a big smile.

Serenity was beautiful, she had long straight black hair with a thin body, long legs and very shapely in between. Greater than her beauty was her intellect, she observed much, spoke little while understanding everything.

She had opposed many suitors as they did not meet her requirements. The young men were stupid and quite childish, while the older men boring and usually fixed on their wealth. No one had ever spoken to her father as Octavian did. That alone fascinated her, his fearlessness while sitting in a wheelchair.

She was pushing him down one of the long hallways, not really with much speed. Just walking slowly when Octavian told her to stop. She complied and he motioned her to come in front of him, by waving his right hand from back to front.

Then with the same hand he motioned her to come closer to his face. She moved closer but it still was not close enough for Octavian. He motioned to her ear and whispered something in it.

Serenity looked at him for a long second, smiled and pushed him with a strong vigor to his guest suite.

John thanked Scott for bringing Octavian, commanding him to stay until all was completed. With that he was instructed to go to his room.

Mr. G, once alone spoke his thoughts.

"Lord, I don't trust him period, it's obvious he is planning something. I doubt he will kill himself, I suggest we start torturing him, after a brief time he will be begging to make it for you."

John shook his head in a no manner, "Usually I would agree with you, but the stakes are high, if he does do it, then it would be done, without any chances of a different problem arising from your suggestion. Also, I find it a challenge, one man in a wheelchair thinking he can outwit me. Stand up to me." At that he started to laugh.

"In the end, your suggestion is always a possibility, currently playing along is fun. What can he do? It is my planet!"

With that he changed the glass to transparency looking at the jungle just five inches away.

Scott like motto, which he collected, reviewing a different one each day. They were like pep talks to motivate his mind for whatever that day would bring. He had slept well as Lord John Husk's home was furnished with only the finest products and services.

His chip was set to pick a random one each day, fifteen minutes after he had awakened. This was what he heard in his head, "Did it alone…Did it broke…Did it tired…Did it scared…Still doing it."

Scott's mind was full of many varied thoughts, he was feeling guilty about bringing Octavian to Lord Husk. Knowing that at best Octavian might make it back to LaTaFree, with the worst-case scenario never leaving Husk's planet or leaving in a box.

The odd thing was Octavian did not seem worried or fearful about his current situation. Scott thought about his favorite book, The Art of War. Octavian was in enemy territory, outnumbered, and handicapped, still he showed no concern about it. Not only that, but he had also taken control so far in dealing with Lord John Husk. That of course, will not last long, were Scott's feelings.

Thinking about his morning's motivational motto, it truly applied to Octavian, except the part of, did it scared. Scott's review of Octavian's past was full of life and death situations. After so many years and encounters, he must be numb to the precariousness of the current moment.

Lord Husk had requested Scott attend the next meeting between himself and Octavian. He was to meet them for breakfast and then they would all go to John's study to work out the arrangements.

Finally, they were all in his study, there were more people there than the first meeting, except Serenity was absent.

Lord John Husk began, "I hope your accommodations were acceptable, as you stated yesterday, let us go over the arrangements for my..."

Octavian now interrupted him, which was never done to any Lord, "John, I ask that everyone at the last meeting be here and no others than that. There are reasons for every request I have and will be glad to expound when this is resolved."

Then as an after thought, "Thank you." With Octavian giving that look that he expected it to be done at once.

John who would have responded differently if anyone else did what Octavian had done, very calmly responded.

"Everyone except Mr. G and Mr. Howard leave now. Also, contact Serenity and have her join us." He said that to his assistant, finishing with a look at Octavian that implied, anything else. John knew what he wanted, his eyes were on the prize. Real men are in control of their emotions and desires; John was proving that he would not be rattled.

After a few moments of commotion, the room was empty of everyone except those that were there yesterday. In fact, each person resumed their earlier locations, now John looked at Octavian and began.

"I will provide all the resources and people needed for its completion. How long do you expect it to take?"

Octavian just replied with, "No, John that will not work." After that he pulled out a cigarette and lighter.

The room was tense waiting for their Lord's response, "I prefer you call me Lord Husk and there is no smoking in this home. I would hate for thousands to suffer because of this."

Then adding to his statement, "I am sure you do not want that on your conscience."

This was a battle between the two men, Octavian smiled yet it was more of an evil smile and spoke.

"John, millions have died in my name, I personally have killed hundreds, I prefer not to be here, what is a little suffering between friends." With that he lit the cigarette blowing smoke in many directions.

Serenity broke the tension, looking at John Husk while saying.

"Father, may I bring our esteemed guest an ashtray."

John looking at his daughter, his anger then faded and with a smile, thinking how smart his first daughter was, a true offspring of his own greatness.

"Yes, that would be fine."

Then looking at Octavian asked, "Please sir, how would you like to proceed."

"I will create the elixir of extended life for just one person, two doses, figuring you will want me to take one, to prove it is safe. I will not reveal how to create it. I will allow only one person to watch me work, also I will request many resources, most I will not use, this is to keep the formula secret. All my request must be done, honored, and last you must prove to me you are worthy. Also, I will constantly try to talk you out of what you want."

He stopped to look into John's eyes, "You can trust no one now that you are on this path. That is why I wanted the room cleared out. You think this is a gift, I know it is a curse. Dragonfly, who's genius only comes along in a millennium, realized that fact. I was at her death bed when she gave me many secrets. Dragonfly could have easily recreated it and used it on herself, but she understood and apologized for giving it to me. Are you prepared to have everything you love, die. To be left alone, with only memories!"

Lord Husk like challenges, that was how he uncovered some of science's secrets. He responded with a question.

"I am sure you have had pets, and after one passed and you had another." John now paused to create a more dramatic moment.

"Do you love the next less than the former?"

Octavian who had been enjoying himself, his attitude changed and replied.

"John, do you see how fast things transform, people becoming pets, for how could they be equal to someone living hundreds of years. Yes, the ordinary person must mourn many lives that died, and it is hard to do, extremely hard. Now imagine having ten times, fifty times, that pain.

I am sure you have tried to do it yourself, there are many ways to achieve it. The Hermetic Order of the Golden Dawn believed every person had the magical ability derived from their own body to achieve extended life."

Stopping there and surveying his audience, Octavian turned to Scott.

"Do you know what I am referring to and if yes please describe."

Scott's first thoughts were why was he being brought into this; everyone was now looking at him, so he began.

"Well, I am no expert on that subject, it was founded in the late eighteenth or early nineteenth century. At one point had many famous people associated with it."

Octavian smiled again and continued, "Why do you think they called it the Golden Dawn?" Now without waiting he continued.

"Because they believed that taking one's urine at dawn was the key to transforming it into what was needed for a long life. Then it would be filtered and stored, heated, and filtered repeatedly, stored for up to three to five years and then the final transformation would begin before it would be consumed.

But there are many ways, Dragonfly used Red Mercury in conjunction with the Philosopher's Stone to create it. Atlantis used a certain gem with periodical usages could give them up to ten thousand years.

My point is there are numerous ways to achieve the result, yet each way is extremely difficult. Imagine having a banquet with one thousand guests, and each dish had to be served at the same moment, with each being perfect from the appetizers to deserts. And if just one dish was just a tiny bit off, barely noticeable but not perfect the banquet would be considered a failure.

What I am going to do is much harder than that banquet, as I had said, if it were easy, you would have already created it."

Serenity reentered the room; with an ornate ashtray and a device it was attached to. She walked over to Octavian, bent her knees, her head horizontal to his. She attached the device onto his wheelchair, then taking both her hands and wrapping them around his right hand gently led it to the ashtray and bumped it. The ashes fell inside, her eyes locked onto his, making Octavian think they were saying, please do not anger father. She left him with a small smile and returned to her father's side.

Lord Husk looking at Octavian spoke, "I will provide all you need and abide by your requirements, I have only one question, how long before it will be ready?"

"John, I honestly do not know, I never tried to recreate it. There will be many tests to make sure it is safe. What needs to happen is transforming elements to create something that is not natural. It takes a lot of energy or time or both. Dragonfly initially did it by chemistry but later refined it to the quantum level. That really was where her true genius shined above all others. Also, I know the formulas and other things needed but do not utterly understand it. The chip in my head does and if not for that, I could not do it. Like an artist, sculptor, or surgeon, I will need time to get my timing and skill right."

Lord Husk appeared to accept that answer, as it felt honest. When dealing with the unknown there are many factors having to come into place at the right moment for success.

The meeting ended with Octavian making lists of items needed and seeing the laboratory he would be using.

Octavian was in deep thought when Scott entered the large laboratory, equipment was being setup while other materials stored against an open wall.

"Looks like they have everything you need, and this is a very impressive laboratory." Scott said proudly, while trying to smile. Thinking to himself, he really needed to work on his smile.

"Rubbish, Earth's technology has been stunted, in fact, its going backwards compared to one hundred years ago. Obviously, the lack of sharing scientific knowledge between cities and lords, combined with the lack of quality education of the general populations. All ending with an obscene amount of control leads to stifling new sciences, I will need to contact others to get all I need." Octavian finished with a look of disgust and disappointment.

"Would you like me to contact Lord Husk with your new requests?" Scott offered.

"No, I can handle that and will go over the costs of such things, I imagine he will soon want a report of my progress." Octavian ended there, leaving Scott with more questions than answers.

How will he get his communications out, the Lords are extremely strict about outside communications, especially on owned planets. Scott's mind had been in overdrive lately, to him Octavian must be planning something. Yet no matter how he envisioned it, and that was the problem, he could not imagine how Octavian could do it.

Then his mind remembered a quote from Albert Einstein, imagination is more important than knowledge. The quote was longer, but that first line summed up its meaning. Scott realizing that his imagination, even with his job as a researcher, was not where it needed to be.

Scott's intuition felt alive now, like it had been in a long slumber and finally had waken, wanting to provide as much information as it could. Octavian not only was planning something but was already getting items in place. Also, Lord Husk must realize that and like himself cannot imagine how he could be defeated.

Deep down in his mind's thoughts, somehow his part was still to come.

—-

Mr. G was not a physical man, he had a beer belly with a shallow chest, his head look larger than most, none of that mattered for it was his mind that shined. He was a general's general, a strategist, a man who could see past the next turn or hill they were at.

He spoke few words and when spoken they were always just above a whisper. Never smiling, he did wear two necklaces, other than that his glasses finished the picture.

Currently he was advising Lord Husk on a variety of issues. Ending with his warning again concerning Octavian.

"Lord Husk, we agree that Octavian will never leave here, even after we gain the potion, formula, and ability to create it on our own. His insolence must be punished, in the end he will show respect to you, Lord."

All rich people end up with slaves, some because they idolize their masters, while others can not imagine their life without being ruled. Serenity had two that would do anything for her, including die for their queen. That type of devotion can be hard for some to understand, though history's past proved it does exist and was plentiful.

Two males' servants that loved her entirely with nothing being too great to do for their queen, Serenity. That is the power of money and fame. It is an aphrodisiac to some, that type of power can be more than most can handle.

Serenity had big dreams, way past father's vision for her life. No matter how great someone was, being in the right place and time, fate was always a part of making that greatness. She was aware that she would not have even been a part of the second meeting if not for Octavian requesting her presence.

She liked him, he was brave but also seemed foolish, her father was extremely powerful. John's mind now focused on people not science, she had seen him break many, even had Lords bend to his will.

On the second day of Octavian's official start, Lord Husk demanded a meeting in his study. Because of that Octavian demanded the Scott and Serenity also be there. To Scott after hearing about it, thought, I am dealing with two control maniacs. After one demanded something the other also has a demand to match it.

For his part, Lord John Husk had been and still was being incredibly patient and tolerant, thought Scott. Of course, eventually that will run out.

"Mr. Octavian, I would like to address some of the requests you have made, your current focus and how long you feel it will take. As in all things, there is limited time for results."

Octavian liked to annoy Lord Husk, he always addressed him by his first name, without any title before it. Also, starting most conversations being defiant when it was not needed.

"John, regarding my requests, which I was also going to address with you. I had no idea that Earth plus your world were so behind in technology. I had to order some equipment, it will be coming soon, please do not have your people touch it. They may damage it, which will only delay what you want. I am sure they will not understand it."

At that point John, started to question him, "What type of technology are you referring to? I have the best scientists not to mention I also am well versed in many areas.

Octavian replied, "You are quite behind in quantum mechanics, especially applied applications, for example creating quantum tunneling, quantum bubbles, plus other areas. I had to spend a sizable amount of funds to make it happen. Your monopoly credit money has no value in the galaxy. Bottom line, you already owe me, so if I ask for a comic book or anything else, I expect to get it!"

It felt genuine, Octavian's hostility; there was not a sound in the room.

Then his mood changed, and he began again in a gentle tone.

"Please, I will share with you some powerful secrets, that will make your name legendary, if you agree to forget this venture. Imagine everything being boring, no surprises, things repeat so often, nothing new. The soul aches for one more day, it is the body that thankfully gives it a final rest. And then there are the changes, every hundred years so many changes. Not to mention that the body is just a container, it can break. I sit here in a wheelchair, it could even be worse for you, that is the thing, with so much time, nothing is certain. Your worst fears can become a reality and then last for hundreds of years."

Again, after Octavian stopped speaking there was absolute silence.

Lord Husk, calmly asked, "How did you send messages out for more equipment?"

"As I have said you are severely lacking in quantum applications. I have been sending and receiving messages thru quantum entanglement via the chip in my head. Imagine two phones that are always connected, and nothing can stop their communications. The chip acts like one end and it is connected to a hub that works the other end. The equipment coming is crucial in completing your request."

John Husk was a smart man, a good man yet being secluded within one's personal bubble, no matter how safe and pleasant it feels, leads to a false sense of grandeur and security. It was at that moment he realized his mistake.

This old man in a wheelchair was much more than he projected. If he could do that, what else was he hiding? Smart people are impressed with other smart people, John now realizing he had a real opponent, someone he would have to take more seriously.

John responding, "I will make sure the equipment gets to you untouched." There was a new respect between the men. Like an acknowledgement had been created.

Octavian then said, "John, I am luckier than you, being able to kill myself on demand is a blessing. I have always been fearful of being trapped in a prison. Stuck there for hundreds of years. That would never happen to me, it could happen to you. The future cannot be predicted, it is just probabilities, you never know, it could happen to you. Again, I will share wonderful technology if you give up this request you ask of me."

Lord Husk now somber, "I will let you get back to your work, do you have an approximation of how long.

"Definitely two weeks, possibly three. It depends on how fast the equipment plus all my requests arrive. All that is based on, if everything goes right, which I highly doubt will happen." Octavian answered.

The laboratory was far from John's study, so when Serenity offered to push Octavian back, he granted her request. She was fascinated with Octavian, which her father understood. There were few like him, even in a wheelchair there was a feeling of power around him.

Five days had passed, Mr. G, the scientist who was helping Octavian and Lord Husk were discussing the progress that had been made.

The scientist explained that Octavian would do experiments in multiple areas, sound and light waves, chemistry, plus his quantum experiments. There were more areas that made no sense, the planet's alignment to other astronomical bodies, weather, holidays that are locally celebrated. Then he played with the computers doing a lot of mathematical formulas, even playing with devices that generated smoke.

Mr. G's assessment was it was all distractions; he questioned whether Octavian could create what was needed. Dragonfly had created it and given it to him, it had never been recorded that he created it for anyone else. Believing that everything he was performing were just distractions.

There was one nagging question that both Mr. G and Lord Husk had, why did he agree to come. Surely, he must had presumed there might be trouble, what gain could he possible have by accepting.

Lord Husk was quiet, listening and thinking, finally he asked the scientist, "Do you think he is making progress? Has he done any testing on animals?" John had been busy with business matters plus two uprisings in two different cities he owned.

"He has not done any animal testing, I really can not determine his progress, he refuses to answer questions. He does talk to himself and lately seems pleased with the results.

Lord Husk then asked, "What does he spend the most time with?"

"His crystals, half the experiments involve them." The scientist responded without hesitation.

He was dismissed; Lord Husk turned to Mr. G and spoke.

"I will give him two more weeks after that I will do as you advised. I know he is planning something, which does not worry me. If he can create it, that will be worth all his arrogance. Stopping him right now just feels wrong. Two weeks, my friend."

Octavian had allowed Scott to watch as he worked in his laboratory. Spending substantial amounts of time there, with the rest in his room or out by the courtyard. Apprehension about time running out was on his mind, which he tried to create a sense of urgency in Octavian.

"My friend, Lord Husk has shown great patience which I fear will run out shortly. I am not trying to rush you, yet hope you are clearly aware of what failure may bring."

"I understand your concerns, things are almost ready, I am waiting on the weather reports. I am looking for a certain condition."

That answer did not rest Scott's trepidation, he wondered if it was an honest answer and if so, what type of weather conditions was he looking for. Or was he just treating him like a fool, figuring I could not tell the difference between real and fiction.

Serenity started to visit Octavian often, always at night after all had dined. Father liked big dinners with many guests, Octavian and Scott had become guest there. Dinners were formally held in dress and conversations.

Octavian was always on his best behavior during those events, keeping a low profile.

"I have great news, please have the usual people attend, I would like to tell John personally." Was the message Serenity heard from Octavian. They were in the courtyard; it was obvious they enjoyed each other's company.

Octavian like the twilight between day and night, Serenity enjoyed his stories, he had one for any type of event a person might experience.

They all met in Lord Husk's study; everyone now had their favorite spots. The chair in front of John's desk had been set aside, ready for Octavian's wheelchair.

"John, I would like to tell you a story, hopefully it will change your mind, if not then we will go over what is needed for your transformation. I have told no one about my time with the First People. They have a class system, the lower the number the greater the honor. To achieve level five, they created nine groups each with nine people in each group. Then they fight to the death, each of the winners were given time to rest. After that, all nine winners, fight to the death. The champion of that fight gets the honor of reaching level five."

The room was silent; Octavian had paused but continued.

"There are things that will happen because time makes it that way. Actions you do, even if there were no regrets, that still will sadden you. It may seem like that story was about savages, animals, people who are just cruel. Yet once utterly understood, everything changes. First, you must kill eight people, your friends. After that kill eight warriors, people who had already proved themselves. And when only one life was left, he receives the honor of level five."

Again, he paused, then said, "Let me ask you, if you were in a fight, outnumbered, the First People love being outnumbered, and you had to choose a fighter to stand by your side. Knowing that there was only one at level five, with the rest at levels six and higher.

Now that savagery would be your best choice, the First People have existed for so long, others have no right to judge them."

At that pause Lord Husk asked, "What level did you make?"

"Level four, and I will not describe any of it, all I will say is it was much harder to achieve then level five."

Lord Husk, who was trying to be patient even with Octavian story telling ask, "So what is the point of your story, why does it matter to me?"

"It is not just all the people that will die before you, time will cause you to perform actions you will either regret or at best, justify, either way they will sadden you. Most only must live with it for possibly sixty years. I have thoughts that go back one hundred and fifty years.

Death is not the enemy, that is one of the things the First People taught me. A worthless life without honor is death each day. You think, you will never be like me, I say time can change many things, I am trying to help you. Again, I will give you something else, a great new science just forget this."

Lord Husk was not impressed with Octavian's words, which he made known.

"With more time, I will create many things, reveal new discoveries in science on my own. What I need from you is more time and nothing else. When will it be ready?"

Octavian had not taken his gaze from John, "It could be ready in a few hours, but I have plans for how it will be given to you. In five days, there is a conjunction between a meteor shower and a storm. I want to perform the final steps outside in an arena, this is a special moment, the sky should reflect that as the wind and rain roar..."

It appeared Octavian had more to say but John's disapproval would not be contained.

"No, I am aware of your habit of double-crossing people you are dealing with. In fact, it is quite apparent you are planning something. I have been extremely patient while providing all you have asked for. Now I demand it be done as soon as possible. A lot can happen in five days."

Octavian looking displeased spoke, "John, this is your planet, you have hundreds of people to protect you and plenty of weapons, yet you fear one old man in a wheelchair. I told you when we started this, that I would only give it to someone worthy. I am extremely disappointed in you."

He then made a gesture with his right hand, with his thumb and forefinger so close together without touching and spoke.

"You are this close to getting what you want! John, we both know you will not let me leave. Once you have taken the elixir, you will want to keep me for ten or twenty years to make sure it is working. Then you will also want the formula, in the end, you will keep me prisoner for the rest of my life."

Then looking John in his eyes with an evil stare, "It will be done the way I want, or I will not do it at all."

Octavian liked to anger Lord Husk, which was a foolish thing to do. Lords are used to always getting their ways. Never having people stand up to them on any subjects. Death was just one of their options, making life terrible was always on the table, and easy for them to do.

The tension felt unbearable within the study, even the animals beyond the glass watching, could feel it.

A big smile appeared on Lord Husk's face, he was a diplomat, "Well, when you put it that way, okay." He ended his smile with a laugh.

Octavian returned the smile with something that did not look quite right. Thinking to himself, even if I get what I want, the chances of it working are slim. Everything would change in five days.

—-

The phone thrown onto his desk, Mr. G was mad, Lord Husk was handling Octavian all wrong. He should be in prison and tortured daily until he revealed everything. Playing along only empowers him. It was hard for Mr. G to understand, really to accept when such glaring mistakes had been made.

He imagined it to playing with fire, eventually you will burn down your home. His biggest concern or question was why Octavian showed up at all. He must have a plan, backup waiting for orders.

Even then, why jeopardize his own safety, what did he really want from Lord Husk?

Scott was feeling conflicted, even before he visited Octavian, deep down he knew it would not be good for Octavian to join him in seeing Lord Husk. One side of his mind arguing that he barely even asked him to come. It was Octavian's decision; Scott had not promised or threaten him in any way.

The other side loudly proclaiming, you did not warn him while also being the cause of his current condition. Then a quiet voice inside his head asked, what can I do?

Octavian was extremely involved in what he now had labeled the Transformation. He wanted a circle surrounded by pillars, each six feet apart. He was very precise in exactly what he wanted and the math in making it happen. Its width should be exactly forty-five feet, each pillar seven feet and things of that nature.

As it was being constructed, multiple times he had sections redone as their dimensions were not perfect.

Time was moving quickly; Octavian consumed with the outside construction project while everyone else's tensions were growing.

As the days came closer to the event, the weather had progressively changed from nice to bad. Octavian wanted to begin at twilight, when asked why his response was, this is all about transformation, the same as twilight.

Mr. G had double the people who would be in the actual circle with himself, Lord Husk, and Octavian. Not wanting so many as they would be in each other's way, he also had two hundred people surround the circle. It all was overkill, but he was not taking any chances.

Scott and Serenity were also to be included in the circle. Now having one day before everything was supposed to happen. That day filled with moving the chemistry equipment plus all the other stuff Octavian wanted there. So many varied items brought to the circle, large crystals that looked almost twelve inches in length and at least an inch wide, transported in specially lined baskets.

Serenity that night, prior to the Transformation had asked her father, that she would rather not attend. That came as a surprise to Lord Husk, figuring she was worried about Octavian being harmed or some unpleasant thing of that nature.

From somewhere in the back of his mind, maybe she was worried about her own safety. Octavian's past was filled with much violence, even though now he was not that man. It felt odd, like an omen or sign that he should be more concerned about tomorrow.

For whatever reasons, he had no fear about his own safety, of course the possibility of being poisoned was always there. Octavian did not seem like that type of man, that method was for cowards.

In the end, he granted her request, with reluctance. She always obeyed him, never dishonored or disrespected him. There was an odd feeling that something he had not thought of was happening.

When Octavian called him out for being scared about doing it outside, that had affected him. Making John want to prove that nothing about tomorrow intimidated his being.

It was not just the static electricity in the air, the anticipation of what was coming in less than one hour had its own power. Still not raining; there were flashes of lightning in the sky which gave the whole affair an ominous feeling. The wind had a constant breeze with gusts that had an extra thirty to fifty miles behind it.

The sky now was turning colors as the twilight had just begun. The arena was surrounded by the columns of stones. There were fires on the tops of the columns with the crystals five feet from the top on the backside of the pillars, that faced outside the circle. It had a very ancient appearance, making the entire event more special.

At one area near the edge within the circle was a throne-style chair for Lord Husk. There also was a small alter near the chemistry set and many diverse items at the other end of the circle opposite from Lord Husk.

John entered the circle with fourteen men plus Mr. G. Outside the circle were over one hundred and fifty people that surrounded it.

There also were four battle androids in the circle, everyone was getting settled down within their spots. Scott was also there near John's seat, once Lord Husk had sat down, a group of people on each side of him formed a V with John at the back point. They could easily protect him while he had a full view of what was happening.

Night was approaching quickly while Octavian was working with the chemistry equipment. The table was set low, so his wheelchair was at the right level for his actions.

The weather was picking up with the winds gusting often by that time. The lightning flashing more often with the feeling of rain just moments away. Octavian was watching the sky when he motioned with his arm, a finger pointing up to mark the meteor shower.

There running thru the sky were small bright lights arching across the night. A couple veering towards the ground.

Octavian was still busy preparing the extended-life potion when suddenly the quartz crystals lit up. A two-foot force field was created that ran around the stone pillars. It ended at the top in an arch that created a dome. Everyone inside the circle could not get out while all the people outside could not get in.

Then a second later an explosion occurred where Octavian was working. A blue-purple mist appeared right where he was at, it being so thick he instantly disappeared within it. The mist started to expand moving from its initial position to the remaining area in the circle. It acted like waves, now slowly filling the space while losing its opaque properties.

Lord Husk was furious, shouting at his men, "Bring him to me, now!"

As the men started to move, Octavian's wheelchair came rolling into their view, slowing down quickly, it was empty.

Then the shooting began, with Octavian going after the battle androids. He was standing with a quartz crystal in the shape of a stick that looked remarkably similar to a magician's wand. It was only a half inch wide and ten inches long.

The blast it produced was astounding, a 4-inch circular laser beam that cut thru personal force fields like a knife busting balloons. Everyone started shooting in that direction, by this point the mist had faded. Octavian was blinking in laser lights; there were also guns firing at him.

Unknown to his enemies, he was wearing a personal forcefield created by Dragonfly with time-crystals. That technology creates unlimited power, like a battery that never empties. It was a gift to his late wife Lilith from Dragonfly, looking like a neckless with an indigo crystal. It was set to block fast moving objects plus energy weapons but if moved at normal speed allowed all actions.

At first, he had destroyed all the battle androids, with three men also killed in collateral damage. Octavian had worked his way opposite of John's throne. Standing thirty feet away he dropped his crystal stick and now pulled out a Roman's short sword. It had a length of fifteen inches, with sharp edges on both sides ending in a point at the end. The perfect weapon for what he was now going to do.

With the sword in his right hand, his left hand's palm was open with four fingers moving inwards. The universal sign to bring it on, Octavian was ready to fight.

Five men walked towards him, spreading out so they would be able to attack from all sides at once.

Scott thoughts were, it was impressive so far, but without his laser weapon there was no chance of beating all these men. Even with his sword, there were just too many. It would only be a matter of time before Octavian's downfall.

The men walked slowly towards him, with one man stopping directly in front of Octavian, two others were to his right and left both about three feet from their target. The last two men were four feet from Octavian parallel to each of his arms.

He had perfected a front kick that was unstoppable if you were within arms length. The only part of his body that moved was his leg with the kneecap its victim, the target. This would jerk the subject forward where his hands would take over.

Octavian without saying a word, struck the man in front of him with his leg, hitting him below the knee. That jerk him forward with the next blow to his eyes, a left hand in claw mode poked extremely hard catching one of his eyeballs.

The man to Octavian's right with his left hand stabbed him below the shoulder. The force was so great it stayed imbedded in Octavian. He turned and moved the sword under his arm and behind his body, puncturing his attacker's lung.

As Scott watched, one of the things that was horrific was his smile. Octavian had been smiling the entire time. Even when he became injured, his smile grew as he turned and put his sword into the man's chest. Another aspect was his calm demeanor, where everyone else had tight faces and were jerkier in their movements, Octavian was relaxed and appeared enjoying himself, without fear of injury or death.

After striking the man in the chest, he turned his attention to the three men who were left. As one of the men approached with what resembled a hammer, Octavian went down to his knees, striking his thighs and groan area. Then rolling on the ground and rising in a different place then before. It was done quickly giving him distance from the last two attackers that were still uninjured.

His plan being to injure them first and then kill them later. He was close to the man with the bad lung who was on his knees when Octavian plowed his sword into his head. The next kill was the man with the injured groin. The man who he had blinded was still having problems, so Octavian then attacked one of the two left unhurt.

Scott now thinking, he must be on drugs, his energy was off the charts. Even with two down, no one could last thru eight more men that were coming.

Mr. G now was getting nervous and in a rare moment, shouted to the rest around his Lord.

"All of you get him, kill him!"

With that the last six men went into action, some had been arming themselves with hand-to-hand weapons. One had a pole type object which he used in his attack.

Most had never seen such carnage or had been in a life and death situation. Sure, Octavian was a great fighter, that now being obvious. Worse was his attitude, taking pleasure in each kill, smiling like he just won an award. It is one thing to survive something like that, yet it is quite another to enjoy it.

As crazy as it appeared, Octavian was doing better when attacked by the full group. Each swing of his sword found a target, as his attackers were in each other's way. There was so much blood now displayed on the ground and each other.

Octavian looked like the devil, a red mass, killing people, smiling, moving, and killing repeatedly. As each man fell, their collective group lost its confidence while Octavian strength appeared to grow.

There were only four men left, two had left the battle too scared to fight, sick with all they had seen and been thru. Trying to hide within whatever was left to take cover and not be killed.

Octavian was closed to one as he was fighting the other two. With what looked like an afterthought, he killed one of the two hiding. There was no mercy in his eyes, no care about his actions, just brutal efficient killing. One strong jab in the man's throat. It was not an instant kill, but death would follow.

By this time, all the fighters were wounded, now having more time plus a view of what was left in front of them. The pain filtered into their minds. Octavian's strategy changed dramatically as he fought. Now with many fighters against him, he would charge quickly ahead, then spin around wounding an enemy trying to sneak up on him.

At times he would make a quick move to the right or left to only then go the opposite direction. This would cause men to crash into each other allowing him to injure someone else.

The unbelievable was happening, for the first time it looked like Octavian could win. There were only three men left, and they were all injured. Octavian had many injuries, yet that did not seem to affect him, not like the others he was against.

Now with only three men standing, one hiding and the other two finally realizing that they cannot rely on someone else to get the job done. The last two fighters increased their attack against Octavian.

His movements slowed down giving the last three more respect before their deaths. One man begged him for mercy; he was rewarded with a quick death.

Scott just could not believe Octavian was still alive. There were times during the battle, he swore he was finished. Then Octavian would explode with power or wiggle out right before a fatal blow could occur. When most were injured, the advantage went to Octavian. He had never seen anyone fight like that, not in the movies or hologram.

There were only Mr. G, Lord Husk, and Scott, with his mind now wondering for the first time since he always assumed Octavian would be killed, if now was his turn. Octavian would have a right to do it, I did deceive him, were Scott's thoughts.

Mr. G now walked slowly towards Octavian and loudly spoke.

"We surrender, please…"

Octavian's answer was a swing of his sword from left to right, which looked like a miss. He was aiming at Mr. G's throat. Octavian push the sword into an arch moving down and then returning in an upward direction. That cut Mr. G's stomach wide open, right at the center. His guts hit the ground before he touched it.

Scott now was frozen; Octavian was death personified, and he was next. He had never felt fear that strong, the thought of trying to defend himself was nonexistent. Octavian still had his personal force field, and it was working. Periodically men would shoot him with no effect.

Octavian was twenty feet away and spoke to Lord Husk with the following words.

"John, Dragonfly gave it to me, I never asked for it, that was her decision. I feel that if you want it, you need to take it from me. Like the passing of the torch, to truly give you that feeling you have earned it! Just go to the alter and take it."

Lord John Husk rose from his throne slowly; his face was red with anger, then without looking where the potion was situated, in a full run at his top speed, went straight for Octavian.

Before his charge arrived, Octavian dropped his sword, frozen, waiting to move at the last moment. If that was his plan it did not happen, with the full force of Lord Husk smashing into Octavian and sending him flying against the force field.

He had done so well against all before him, Lord Husk's personal rage plus Octavian tiring out and with all his injuries was not moving. As John approached him, walking slowly with murder in his eyes.

Lord John Husk picked him up by his neck with his large hands pulling Octavian off the ground. His strength made it look like Octavian was a rag doll. He had little time left to live.

Octavian's right arm and hand from the elbow down were previously lost in an earlier fight. It was replaced with an android arm and hand. With his last thought he moved his right arm smashing into John's left arm. The collision broke both men's arms, with Octavian's snapping off at the elbow and John with a compound fracture.

John had a warrior's spirit; it can be hard to define but easy to realize when seen. He disregarded the pain, wiped it out of his mind and slowly leaning over the fallen Octavian resumed with his right hand on his throat.

Scott had been frozen and now was free, feeling as if time had appeared to stop, and he had a flash back to Octavian's housekeeper. Her words now burning in his mind, he could hear them in his ears. Her demand and his response. She said, promise me you will guard him with your life.

A great impulse gripped his being making him act without thought. He looked at his feet, there was an energy gun. Picking it up and without hesitation set it to hard stun firing at Lord Husk. Octavian's personal force field protected most of John's body but not all of it. His head and back received the blast, then his body froze, and he fell over to the right of where Octavian lie.

Scott rushed over to them both, now thinking it was for nothing as Octavian looked gone. First, he patted his face, then panic set in, as his pats turned to slaps. Finally, he awoke struggling to get air. Octavian's neck was damaged, making breathing difficult yet he was alive.

The first words he spoke were, "Come on. Come on do it!"

Scott assuming, he was speaking to him, responded with, "I did all I could, what else can I do?"

"Not you!" As Octavian spoke his attention turned to the magnificent home.

"I am sorry getting you into this, we are both going to die." Scott said solemnly.

"We are not going to die." Replied Octavian with the emphasis on the not. Still, he looked at the home sitting in the distance. The men and women outside the arena still surrounded it.

Scott's thoughts at that moment should have been filled with terror, they were not. He felt good about helping Octavian, even if it only provided a small amount of extra time for him to live. Now he also was looking at the home that sat fifty yards away and above them.

The first explosion was followed and within a second the second bomb then went off. Between both explosions there showed a huge hole within the mansion.

Once that happened Octavian stood up, he now was in bad shape. The fight against the men had left many injuries. Then the punishment from Lord Husk plus the loss of his arm and hand did not leave a pretty sight.

"Time to go!"

Scott now looking at him like he was crazy, "There are hundreds of people around this circle, we can't fight our way out!"

Octavian stood there with his eyes closed and within an instant the force field had disappeared and within less than a second from that the laser lights had now moved in a crisscross pattern killing everyone around the circle.

With Scott's help and Octavian's good arm around his neck for support they left the arena and traveled down towards the pond.

Chaos was heard everywhere, shouting as the home was burning. Then screams of survivors when they saw all the bodies left at the circle.

Scott still was thinking how could they survive. Stuck on this planet, when order finally prevails, they will be hunted down and killed. Octavian was directing him to a spot only he knew. It was dark and he wondered how he even knew where to go.

Flares were now being shot into the black night sky, slowly sinking down to the ground. Octavian was very aware of his surroundings, when light appeared above them, he saw what he was looking for. Fifteen yards from the pond sat two boulders with one appearing more beat up then the other.

"Go that way." Was Octavian's directions, as they approached the rocks, Scott had a huge surprise.

"Father, one of the ships is damaged, we only have three seats." There were the man and woman from Octavian's home in LaTaFree. She watched Octavian's face for what he wanted done.

Before he replied, the young man looked at Octavian, no words were spoken.

Then Octavian commanded, "Time to go!" His focus was on the woman. Moving on his own without Scott's help towards the rock in better shape. The woman looked at her husband then turned and followed Octavian.

Scott thinking, what was it with being around Octavian that made people want to risk their lives in saving him. He had just done that very thing, now both people who lived with Octavian also were risking theirs. He imagined all the people in the past that had done the same.

Yes, Octavian was special, truly one of a kind yet it felt like something greater than that. A grand design that needed him around and it was others jobs to make sure it happened. He knew the man and woman who came to rescue them were married, she never looked back, her only concern was for Octavian's well-being. That type of devotion had its own beauty, strength in believing so greatly in your cause that nothing else mattered.

The ship was tiny, having only two seats and a small backspace for storage. The woman had taken the pilot's seat and Octavian the space next to it. Scott struggled to fit in the back, after sucking his breath in, squeezing as tight as he thought possible, the door shut.

With the use of anti-gravity propulsion, in less than a minute they were in space. Docking with a star-ship they made a jump, heading towards the planet LaTaFree.

After arriving there Octavian, was rushed to their medical center. The next day he was back in his home, a new android arm and hand, with medical orders to have prolong rest. Most of his stab wounds and bruises were not serious, the one in his back just below his collarbone was not good but with time healed.

3

QUESTIONS AND ANSWERS

They were back in his study, Scott remembering the first time he was there. So many things had changed since then.

"I have so many questions." Scott said that with his best smile. Realizing just then that trying to smile never works, he just had to feel it.

Octavian who was in a jolly mood responding with, "Okay."

Scott began with, "I still am not used to you walking around." Then with a laugh he asked the first of many questions.

"You were smiling the entire time, why?"

Octavian was currently smiling, just like in the battle, "I can tell you don't know the warrior's way. Please realize most don't, even the ones who author books on it. Let me explain it like this. As a warrior you realize your death is never far away. It could happen by something falling from the sky. As a warrior you hope it will be in battle, not because of some other worldly thing that might occur. So, if you are in battle and die, it is still honorable, if you kill others before your death, even better. The point is, you are in the best place you can be, so why would you not be smiling?"

Scott thinking, when it was framed like that, it makes sense. Then he kept asking questions.

"Why did you not kill everyone with the laser wand?"

"That would be wrong, I only wanted to use it on the battle androids. When it came to the men, I was outnumbered yet had a sword, that felt fair." Octavian answered.

"The biggest question, but I have more, why did you go in the first place. You knew it was a trap." Scott now looking right at Octavian's eyes.

With a big smile and little laugh, like it was the most obvious thing that did not even require an answer.

"You, I knew that John would be very displeased if you arrived empty handed."

Scott now trying to process that this man he did not know would risk everything he had just for his benefit.

Octavian seemed to read his thoughts and added, "We both like the book, The Art of War. I needed to be a spy and cross enemy lines, find my enemy's weakness. I chose the time and place of battle. I deceived my enemy in thinking I was weaker than I was, with the wheelchair. Plus, I had a plan of using the crystals before I left."

Scott focusing in on his last statement, "Please explain the whole crystal thing to me."

Octavian usually would question what he knew first but just replied.

"Quartz crystals have special properties, one being they vibrate back and forth thousands of times per second. Watches use crystals to keep time with 32,768 oscillations per second. Now combine that with Time Crystals and bingo you have a magic wand."

Scott was a smart man, inquisitive which led him to be a researcher. Octavian knew so much he was unaware of.

"What are Time Crystals?"

"My mistake, I take it now for granted, Dragonfly had discovered them so long ago, I forget most don't know. She was looking to create a clock with an unlimited power source. Something that could be dependable regardless of changes around it. Her brilliance was in quantum mechanics. She was able to rearrange the electrons and protons within crystals so that all the electrons were on one side while all the protons were on the other. Then they started rotating, each column moving to the other side. That never stops, no power was needed to maintain its movement. Up and down, each side, the electrons in one group and the protons in the other. Then take that movement and multiply it with each little vibration a quartz crystal has, which multiplies the power. What you are left with is a battery that will never run out, unlimited power depending on the size of the crystal and its oscillation rate."

Octavian now acting like it was completely answered.

Scott asked, "Do you think Lord Husk, will ever get over it?"

"No. John is not the same man he was and will never be that man again. He wasn't a bad person, just greedy regarding time. He was always a warrior just not aware of it. After my contact, I have changed him, now an angry dangerous warrior who will never rest until he has his revenge. John and I will meet again, it is destined, only one will leave from that next encounter."

Then Octavian looking at Scott and offered, "You are welcome to stay here and of course free to leave if and whenever you desire."

At that moment there was a knock on the door. Scott fearing the worst was laughing at himself when it was only the children, wanting One to go play with them.

As the days passed, Scott kept asking questions about what had happened.

"How did you know Serenity would keep her word and not betray you?'

"I explained to her the power of cooperation." Looking at Scott, Octavian continued.

"Say you have something I want, and I have something you want. But neither of us will know if the other will give the real thing or deceive. With that in mind there are four scenarios. We could deceive each other, and we both lose. Each could deceive the other with the person being deceived, losing. Or we can both provide what the other needs and we both win."

Scott pressed the issue, "What about if she did trick you, what would have happened?"

Octavian looking hard at Scott, an evaluation stare and spoke.

"I made a judgment call, she really needed what I had to offer, she had more to lose than I did. We still would have escaped; I always have a back up plan. Her part was not that important, just made things easier, not having any planet defenses as we left. She was to destroy their command center. I told her after that to get on a star-ship and head into deep space with multiple jumps. After eighty years no one will care when she makes her reappearance. Serenity at her age should last a thousand years."

Scott then returning Octavian's look asked, "Did you retake the elixir?"

For the first time, Octavian's smiled faded a bit, "You ask a lot of questions." With a bigger smile than before and said, "Yes, I had to know if it would work, in my case it won't matter as I am already so old. The beauty of extended life is having it when you are young."

The days turned into weeks; Scott and Octavian talked about many varied subjects. There were times he did not know if Octavian was just making things up. He would be so positive about areas he could have no possible direct knowledge of. His recovery went quickly with the wound behind his shoulder blade taking the longest amount of time to heal.

Scott wanted to document Octavian's current life and then author a book about it.

As he tried to sell the idea to him, his mind played it back in his memory.

Imagine *Octavian Tales*, so what do you think?

Octavian who did not look initially pleased then responded, Okay, with one condition.

That was one aspect about him, he always liked to take control of situations with his conditions. In that case it was no problem if it was after his death. Scott had protested with the logical conclusion that he would die before him.

Yet from Octavian's view, there was nothing guaranteeing that. The possibility of his passing from something could occur any moment of any day.

Scott had accepted the conditions with mixed feelings. He really wanted to see it published yet never wanted his friend to die. When he expressed that to Octavian, he moved his head in total agreement saying it was one of the conundrums of life.

Months had passed and in Scott's mind the episode with Lord Husk felt surreal. Octavian did like his former arm and hand better, which he missed. Created by Dragonfly, his love for her would allow no replacement to be suitable.

There can be no greater pleasure than living in LaTaFree, between its examples of all things beautiful from flowers, paintings, music and so much more. Also, understanding with appreciation the unique qualities of different life forms. That was just one aspect of its culture, whatever you wanted, could be reached within its borders.

They were sitting at the back porch, which was similar to the front door porch without a walkway leading to it. Having the benefit of more privacy given the surrounding hills that enveloped it.

Scott was talking about properties of light when Octavian said.

"You realize everything is light, just fields that hold and make things look different."

Scott replied, "So you think people can be beamed up thru a house via a light beam."

Octavian looked surprised, "Of course, it has been done to me multiple times. The light they use makes all the other lights merge with its vibration, once all are matched it is retracted back to the source, turned off and there you are."

4

YELLOW SPACE

Their discussion was interrupted with knocking at the front door. Both men went to answer it, Scott still very apprehensive that Lord Husk would attack them at any moment. Octavian opened the door to find a noticeably young man, dressed in his finest clothes. He bowed when he saw Octavian, who had not moved since the door opened. Then he put his hand out to shake whoever had come to visit. If bowing was not enough, the visitor had taken his hand and kissed it.

Octavian motioned for him to sit and begin to speak.

"Hello, my friend, please who are you and why do I have the pleasure of your visit?"

"Thank you, great Octavian for hearing my request, the Council of Nine needs your help for a problem I cannot express, as they did not tell me. It is imperative you visit them as soon as possible. On a personal note, thank you, I am aware of the Final Battle, it is an honor to be here."

"I will leave today in a few hours, okay?" Octavian ending with a big smile.

Scott now interjected, "Yes, whenever you are ready, Octavian, so am I." It was said with authority, making it plain he wanted to come.

The young visitor elated replied, "I have a ship waiting for our departure. Thank you, so much great Octavian, and to your friend."

Octavian then spoke, "As long as you stop calling me great!" There was no smile to accompany it.

"Of course." With his head bow slightly, the huge smile could not be masked on his face. He was invited inside yet insisted on waiting at the porch.

Scott had mixed feelings about the whole affair, recently in his past, he was that young man, who desperately needed Octavian's help. Now, he wanted to say, go away.

Also, seeing Octavian in action he well understood his effect on people. Just the way the young visitor treated him with such high respect. It was hard not to compare one's life to his, with most things never being as grand or big and especially as meaningful.

During his time, he had many different wives, children, experiences, led the battle to save the galaxy and so much more. Most will never even know what happened on Husk's world.

Scott had heard of the Council of Nine, the reality of meeting them shortly was so exciting. By this point, not having Octavian in his world would feel wrong.

They went to a less traveled area that handled departures. There was a shuttle waiting to take them to the star-ship it departed from.

No passes needed or check in required, the longer he was away from Earth the more he saw it for the prison it had become. Realizing how much control was used on its citizens, overkill when it was not necessary.

His worries about the chip installed in his head being manipulated or something worse, never happened. For the first time in his life, he felt free. Thinking about the article he wrote on Octavian and how foolish it was.

The ship was nicer than the earlier transports he had taken. In less than fifteen minutes they were on the star-ship.

Scott had never seen such a huge craft, it was a city in space, with everything cities have. They were escorted to a briefing room, where the council was waiting.

To Scott's disappointment the entire group were not there. Only four greeted them, most he had heard about, yet it is different when seeing something in person.

There was the Praying Mantis, two Tall Whites, a Dragon man, and something that was very foreign to a human form, looking like a pool of water.

Initially it felt like nothing was happening, then everyone started to talk. Unbeknownst to Scott, Octavian and the others were using mental telepathy when Octavian demanded they all talk with sound.

Octavian then paraphrased the information that had previously been exchanged.

"A yellow hole has appeared in space, and it is slowly expanding. Everyone and everything sent into it has not returned, also no information has been discovered on what is inside it. That pretty much sums it up."

With that Octavian was looking at the Praying Mantis, who then began to speak.

"Yes, even the First People entered it and never returned. We feel because of your chip we might be able to devise a plan for your return. The First People refused to allow us to try, we are hoping you will agree."

At this point Scott with accusation in his voice, "You're asking him to go on a suicide mission. There must be another way!"

Octavian then spoke, "Please allow me a moment of privacy with my friend." With that they moved over to a corner of the large room.

"They would not be asking me if they were not desperate. They sent negotiators, politicians, soldiers, and multiple combinations of each. They don't know what else to do if they do nothing and it keeps growing?" Looking at Scott with a concern face.

"Can I deny the universe when it asks for my help? In my past I had to get into a pyramid that was impossible to enter. Now I must enter a space impossible to leave. It is my destiny."

They resumed their spots within the group and the Praying Mantis continued.

"As soon as you enter, leave and return. Those actions are extremely important. We are ready to prep you for your journey. May your return be swift and safe."

Scott watched Octavian, the man just never looked like he was afraid. Each creature thanked him personally, then led him to the prepping area for the journey into the yellow hole in space.

They boarded an exceptionally large shuttle that had small shuttles within it. The yellow hole did not have any gravitational effects to speak of, making it safe to get quite near it.

Octavian did not want to take any weapons with him, not even his short Roman sword, which he loved. He did take his personal force field which sat around his neck. He had a smile on his face as he boarded the personal shuttle.

Scott now thinking about the irony that Octavian would outlive him. Knowing how he lives, it was always a fifty fifty chance. Now the odds looking better for his *Octavian Tales* to become published.

He had not offered to go with him; Octavian's chip was key to getting him home. Only Octavian and the First People had them, making an offer useless. Yet, watching him risk his life, while others just wait, ate at his soul. He was extremely impressed with Octavian but truly did not think he would be returning from this.

They watched as Octavian's craft approached the yellow hole, his speed was constant when he entered it. From the perspective of the people watching, his ship completely disappeared, the instant it broke the threshold.

It was similar to a space jump yet different, the former had stars that seemed to stretch with the latter having a tunnel of colors. A rainbow spinning in a clockwise direction while also curving from left to right and up and down.

Octavian wondered what he would encounter, the good news, he was still alive. Relaxing and enjoying the light show, laughing within, and asking himself why do people always expect the worst?

The ship's controls were nonfunctional; Octavian's spirits were good while also getting bored of the rainbow tunnel. After what felt much longer than it actually was, then again who can really judge time. Even clocks are effective by outside forces. Octavian had spent his whole life thinking about time. The invisible hands that controlled all things.

Eventually the movement felt slower with the colors velocity now almost stopping. When he came out of the tunnel his ship automatically landed. He had no control over the vessel; it lent to his spirits letting go.

Feeling it was a sign, how the ship landed by itself, without the need of intervention. He would take things as he sees them. A thought came to him and left as quickly as it appeared in his mind. The Council of Nine wanted him to now try and return home. He could see the tunnel he had exited from. It was huge, much larger than in his home universe.

The thought of getting back into the ship and trying just felt wrong. It was hard to explain even to himself. There were much greater secrets waiting to be discovered and leaving now was the coward's way.

He would explore this land, and when ready return to his ship and report back, that was the plan.

Located on a hill with a valley below his view, he saw a medieval village before him. The sun laid low to the horizon with fires already lit in some of the areas below.

As he traveled down the path, it felt like when in a dream, as your body never has weight during that time. Every few steps brought him 3 to 5 yards closer, at least that is the way it felt. Also, like dreaming, there was no tiredness. Within minutes he was approaching the beginning of their civilization. There were fires that lined the path making most things visible in the semi-dark.

A group of children rushed up to him, one said, "They told us you would be arriving soon, there is going to be a banquet tomorrow. Will you tell us one of your tales, please." As the child said that the remaining members agreed with the speaker saying, please and the rest echoing all at the same time that request.

Flooded with requests to speak, which is easy to do for most, especially when others want to hear what you are saying. He told them about the time he was in Antarctica exploring a pyramid under the ice. That he traveled into the 4th dimension, into a tesseract. The children looked puzzled, so he explained it is a specific type of hypercube that is in the 4th dimension. Finally, saying it was bigger on the inside then the outside, which cleared it up for everyone.

After that story, his fans wanted more, with Octavian politely declining. Then something happened that made him believe he had died.

During his battle with General Max, over 100 years ago, Sweetbull a blue nose pit bull was his best friend. She died trying to save him, when that happened, he changed inside. You never get over the death of a close friend. Sweetbull was his best friend and now she was running towards him. She was over ten years old when it happened, now she looked nine months young again.

Sweetbull gave Octavian many kisses, her tail wagging so hard it hurt his thighs when hit. At one point she had toppled him over and would not let him get up. Like all the time between them pend up and now flooded out.

His mind evaluating both sides, seeing Sweetbull, feeling so light and strong, not having any bodily needs like eating, drinking and such things. On the other hand, there was no transition between the events. Not even for one second did anything become uncomfortable or not normal. This explanation would also answer why no one ever returned.

Octavian expected death to hurt, at least until he moved to whatever was next. He thought he would take a different form and feel and think in ways he had never felt before. None of that happened. He thought going back to his ship would confirm what he now believed, his death was permanent.

Sweetbull was directing him, walking in front while constantly looking over her body to make sure Octavian was following. She led him to a magnificent castle, having guards and a drawbridge to finish its appearance.

Everyone knew who he was and added a title he had always wanted. Once long ago in his past he was a captain of the star-ship Nevermore. Which is a great position to have until he heard about his friend, Utago, who then became King Utago. He had always been jealous not of Utago but the title. It was something he had never acquired or if you are really that great a person, given.

They hailed his arrival, blowing horns and proclaiming, "King Octavian has arrived!"

Once Sweetbull and Octavian entered the castle more strange things were revealed. The structure was a mixture of old and new, having wireless electricity while also having many lit flames thru-out. The plumbing was modern, yet the floors and walls felt old.

Octavian thoughts being it was the best of both worlds. This place, whatever its title was marvelous. A spot that you intuitively know you never want to leave. That suits you perfectly and you could never be in a place better than exactly where you are at.

He imagined all those other travelers before him, reaching their perfect place and like himself had no desire or intentions of leaving. In that scenario they are not dead or if they are, it is better than life where they lived before.

There were many within the castle to help with all the tasks needed, from cleaning to cooking, maintenance, plus keeping the fires going and more. They provided a meal before showing him around.

The whole affair felt like it was taken partly from his imagination and partly from what he had read or seen in movies. Even though he felt stronger, reality felt very real. The people he interchanged with had emotions, thoughts, and memories.

Looking at Sweetbull who never left his side, just like she used to do. Octavian's mind still troubled on exactly what had happened. Thinking he might be dead, and all these visions are from his mind.

The food was delicious, the meat served on its own, while other plates had extravagant dishes with many ingredients, the results being incredible. He shared half with Sweetbull, just like the old days.

Also, there were official guests that shared the meal with Octavian. It was like they knew he enjoyed company while eating.

Deep in Octavian's thoughts, there was something nagging in his mind. Like a song title that cannot be named, yet you know it, but unfortunately just can not remember what it was. There were memories in his brain that seemed blocked to all his thoughts.

With all the pleasures he was currently experiencing it felt very unimportant. The feeling that tomorrow will be even more wonderful than today was present within his mind.

His bedroom had a huge fireplace and a large balcony; the wind had picked up with the temperature now better for sleeping, pleasantly cooler. It was as if his subconscious was creating exactly what he liked.

Walking onto the balcony, enjoying the air, its height gave a wide view of all that was below. They told him that tomorrow he would meet El, who would be able to answer all his questions. Later after that, the banquet for his arrival will begin. And then the party afterwards, everyone was happy and playful. They did not use money for their survival, they had committees that handled different areas, such as how much food or electrical quantities were needed in the future.

Understanding that working together to provide all their resources was the best way to achieve harmony. Which was a valued concept to their world order. That was why his arrival was so important, they needed their king.

Octavian had always believed in the equilibrium theory. There is a natural order to balance all properties. A perfect example is how water always finds its level or when something wonderful happens while an awful thing also occurs.

Here the balance felt perfect, people happy, having an innocence that was beautiful.

Leaving the curtains open to the fresh air from the balcony, his sleep was simply wonderful, waking and feeling ten years younger than the night before. The clothes hanging in front of him were richly embroidered with gold threads. Colors featuring blacks, reds, and some purples were plentifully about. After dressing and looking like a cross between a pirate, king, and noble. Octavian had a unique appearance to put it mildly.

The castle was built with stone, having big pictures and curtains plus candles all about it. They had made a breakfast that could only be described as fit for royalty. Eggs Benedict plus many varied dishes displayed. It included Lox and bagels, meat dishes, a fruit tray, plus many types of drinks and breads.

More important to Octavian was his meeting with El than the banquet after that. It was held in the rose courtyard, which was lined on three sides with all distinct types and colors of roses. There were cushioned chairs surrounding a fire pit that were used at nights.

They had placed a large table over the fire pit which was loaded with fruits plus an assortment of drinks. During the meeting only Octavian and El were present.

Octavian was sitting there when the announcement was made that El had arrived and wanted an audience with King Wright.

Jumping out of his chair, as he did not know what the proper procedure was for something like that, Octavian moved to shake her hand.

The staff giggled before they hurried out giving them their privacy.

El had the form of a woman, around 35, with long blondish-red hair, and a beautiful smile. There was a peace within her that radiated about, a wisdom that did not need to show off.

"Thank you, your majesty for this meeting, you truly are everything that has been spoken about you."

Octavian smiling at his guest responded, "Please, we both know who the real power is here. I have many questions."

El smiled back, "Please ask anything you like."

"Am I dead, if yes that is quite alright, considering this place."

"No, you are exactly as you were before you arrived." El answered.

Octavian now seriously asked, "Please explain Sweetbull, is she a copy of the real Sweetbull as she had passed over one hundred years ago."

El who never looked away from his eyes during her answers, "No, she is the only Sweetbull you have ever known. Once I explain this place my answers will make more sense. I am from the 6th dimension; this construct was created so that we can interact with the lower dimensions. If I were to enter your 3rd dimensional space, it would rob me of most of my abilities. This way we can interact in a mutual space without limitations. In fact, you have many more abilities than before."

Octavian still focusing on his actual existence, "So is this like a dream space, is it real or am I just creating all I see?"

El's smile felt like when a child asks questions that are obvious, "No, this is as real as where you were before you arrived. In that regard, what is real? Even if it was a dreamscape, which it is not, you can feel, think, experience everything as before, what really is the difference?"

Octavian thinking about her question, she was right, if you can not tell the difference between them then there is none.

"Please explain Sweetbull to me?"

"Imagine a song, that you have not heard in a long time, when you do hear it again, exactly as it was before, whether a record or tape or whatever form of media it was stored on. Once you reproduce all the elements needed for its performance, it is what it was before. I have picked Sweetbull out of her other timeline and inserted her here. This space allows for time to move forward or backwards. That is why she looks much younger than when she was last with you."

"Am I free to leave?" Octavian asked.

"Anytime." El answered with a big smile. Octavian, thinking she had the most beautiful smile he had ever seen. His thoughts were all the others that came here, created their personal heavens, and of course would never want to go back, as he also was feeling.

For some reason, his brain went to the question that was on the council's mind.

"Will the hole within my old universe continue to expand?"

"This space is much different, in simple terms incredibly large, we made a tiny pinprick, careful not to disturbed that realm. We had slightly increased its size but have no plans on further expansion of its size or volume. I suggest you enjoy your banquet tonight and we can talk tomorrow about anything you like."

There was live music with also recorded tunes, the kingdom was a mix of old and new, some might say the best of all things. Magicians provided entertainment with comedians and other types of performances held.

Everyone had a drink in hand also with many smoking. The merriment was real; it was everyone's party. Their king seemed kind and had truly few requests forced upon them. He asked everyone to wear a name badge, so he could remember their names better and address each person accordingly.

Also, asking that all attend, though they could leave any time they liked.

After the entertainment and eating there were special people waiting to be announced. The king's table sat on a raised platform overlooking the festivities. The other tables were on the left and right in front of it, with a walkway and area in front of the platform for the entertainers.

Horns were blown before each name was announced. It all was very formal with the first sounding as such.

"The honorable and incredible wise, Dragonfly, bearing wishes of prosperity and gifts for King Wright." After that was spoken there were cheers from the crowd.

Octavian was speechless, his mind trying to interpret all he was experiencing. One of his aids were whispering into his ear, "Say, welcome Dragonfly."

"Welcome, dear Dragonfly, please come and sit near me." Octavian said.

It was all starting to be too much for Octavian to handle. As he spoke to Dragonfly the horns sounded again.

"Captain Bubba Jones, a close friend and honorable man brings good cheer and gifts for King Wright."

"Bubba is here now too, my closest friend, how wonderful!" Octavian was not prepared for what was coming next.

The horns shouted again, the next special guests were ready to be presented.

"Lilith, wife of Octavian, mother of Blanche and our Queen, accompanied by Blanche Wright, daughter of Lilith and our Princess have arrived."

Octavian was shocked, his mouth slightly open, tears started to run down his eyes as he regained his movement and rushed to meet them.

He embraced his wife, Lilith, who hugged him back and whispered, "My little monkey, I am here for you." Then she gave him a kiss as Blanche looked at them both, with the thought, will they never stop. She giggled to herself as her father gave her a hug.

Octavian's world could get no better than now. Reunited with his wife and daughter, best friend, and Dragonfly, who he had a special kindred with.

The next day he looked forward to talking with El, as he had several types of questions this time around.

Waking up to see his kingdom below and having his family by his side, wanting nothing just feeling blessed for all around him. Those thoughts were on Octavian's mind. A perfect dream never wanting to wake up. The longer he was there the more his prior life faded away. Not in the memories, but the significance it had to his current surroundings.

It felt more like a dream and now he was awake with those prior memories but not feeling their importance. The time was approaching noon, when El agreed to arrive, per Octavian's request. They met in the rose courtyard.

El who always looked beautiful had her usual peaceful persona, treating him as if he were true royalty, "Your majesty, whatever I can do to make things better, please let me know? It will be my pleasure to make it so."

Octavian plus his family and friends knew he was no king, with everyone else treating him exactly as if he were.

"I just have some questions; there is nothing more that I need." Octavian felt humbled, sitting before him was the real power to this world, now asking him after providing everything he could wish for, if he wanted more.

El giving him her beautiful smile, Octavian hated to be rushed, no matter if he had over-spoken, El was patient. That aspect was wonderful, making Octavian really relaxed.

Finally, he asked his questions, "How many people could you provide this for, creating their perfect world, making it so they would never want to leave?"

El was short with her words, reminding him of certain people in his past.

"That number is infinite."

Octavian trying to understand with a 3rd dimensional mind, "But would there never be a shortage of resources or space. Some aspect that creates a boundary?"

El just looking at Octavian with a smiling face, "No, there are no boundaries, no limits to what can be created." Then she looked like she was thinking to herself and added.

"The only limitation is imagination, after a long period of time, that can run out."

Octavian thinking they were like fish in a fishbowl, a distraction that makes certain things fun again.

"I have noticed that everyone except my daughter Blanche, and I, look younger than I remember, that effect is very apparent especially with Sweetbull, please explain why?"

El always had looks, this one saying you may not like the answer.

"You could look twenty-five if you wanted to, let me explain Sweetbull first and then you. Sweetbull's spirit is that nine-month-old puppy you adopted. That is how she sees herself, so that is what she has become. Most see themselves in their younger form, now with Blanche her current age is her favorite. You are different, you have grown accustomed to being old because of all the years you had lived that way, it has now become you."

Then added, "You do look younger than when you arrived!" Ending with a giggle.

Octavian laughed and added, "I feel so much better, like I have grown younger on the inside." Then thinking she was right again.

"Is our time here limited to a regular lifespan?"

El responded, "In the 3rd dimension, your lives are so controlled by time, here time is controlled by you. After living a long life and aging you can just reverse the process and become younger and younger again. Death also is an element that does not rule here."

Octavian was hearing her but inside having trouble believing this was all real. A part inside his mind still having issues accepting all the unbelievable fabulous aspects of this land and his life currently.

He still felt like he had forgotten something especially important yet could not think what it was.

Scott was looking at the device, the machine his friend was lying in. It looked like an enlarged round coffin, with one old person as its passenger. There was a security being, a dragon-type person plus three scientists also in the room.

One man had explained the process that Octavian was going thru, Scott, replayed it in his mind. It had to do with quantum entanglement, Octavian's chip made him special. As he explained that no matter how far the distance between two entangle particles, when one has a reaction the other instantaneously does the same. But when time was suspended long enough for a break to happen, then when the second particle was reactivated, the outcome may be different than its companion particle. In that case, the universe only takes the reading of the last particle and erases the history of the first particle.

The scientist went on to explain that it is not known what state the last particle will be in, as when the wave collapses and seen, can be quite different than the former state. If it worked, Octavian would be there and then back again to his other half. Scott had questioned that part and told that he was cloned without his knowledge, entangled with that clone, again without Octavian knowing. Then Octavian was placed into a time capsule with time completely frozen inside. That created the break needed with his clone, and when he is awakened, hopefully his clone will disappear in history and only he will remain alive.

Scott had questioned, if that history disappeared, how will he know it. The answer was even more fuzzy with the *ghost memory* of that event living in the original Octavian. The scientist explained that the Mandela effect could be explained in that way. A memory that happened and never happened and yet you remember it as if it did.

Hopefully, Octavian will explain it more clearly, Scott thought. He had only been in the time lock for five minutes, with two of the scientists wanting to awake him. They were not talking but Scott now able to hear their thoughts as they spoke to each other. One had said, five minutes is plenty of time to break the connection, with one holdout, who must had been important, wanting to wait another few minutes.

After what felt like the longest next five minutes, they started to fiddle with the controls attached to the time-lock chamber. Initially he barely moved but then started trying to get out of the device. When he was standing next to it, Octavian acted like he was drunk, unable to stand on his own. He slumped over to the security guard, falling on top of him.

Octavian had all his senses, with only one purpose in mind. One last mission, where failure would be worse than death. Now, his thoughts leading to a singular action, get the gun from security.

The power of one thought put into action plus having the advantage of surprising your enemy, can achieve what might seem impossible.

Octavian went for the gun, he already was all over the guard, everyone thought it was some side effect from what he had just endured. Once he had the gun in his hand, by this time the guard was strongly struggling to keep it.

His next attention was to the settings on the gun, taking a good punch from the guard that knocked him off his feet.

While on the floor he shot the guard who went straight down to the ground. Getting up quickly, he then without hesitation shot the three scientists.

As Scott watched he was amazed how quickly he pulled the trigger on the scientists. It felt like only one second, or a second and a half. Either way it was fast, just then he saw Octavian looking at him, with his gun in hand. After what felt like an extraordinarily long two seconds, he bolted thru the door.

Scott hesitated for a moment, should he run after Octavians, by the next instant there was a security officer taking him to the command center.

The Preying Mantis was there plus many others. They were standing around a table that projected a holographic image of their current ship, showing Octavian shooting everyone as he approached the shuttles.

Octavian's personal shield was a real game changer, thought Scott. Even though he was shot many times, it never failed to protect him. Also, Scott's thoughts went to the man, Octavian. Unlike so many in power, who have great control over so much, yet do not get directly involved in the action. Octavian had his personal power, which loomed over people around him. When it was needed, he would personally dish it out, whether killing a dozen men or putting his life at risk.

The Mantis was very composed, Scott was happy he could hear what had been said, which was mostly by the Mantis creature.

Octavian had reached a large shuttle and now was trying to get it freed from the docking support, the release usually done by someone in the command center. The one he had chosen was already in space, just attached by a structure to get inside. It was held in place by electromagnetic beams.

Scott felt some things which were not heard but felt by the people around him. There was confidence the beams would hold him, or it was just hope that it would.

By this time, Scott was for Octavian, whatever had happened he wanted to go back, he deserved that and the fact they were trying to stop him was wrong. They later found out that he had set the gun on high stun mode with no one hurt.

The shuttles engines went into full acceleration while Octavian also had the brakes on. When the power was at its maximum, he released the brakes. There was a great battle between the holding beams and the ship's velocity that lasted a few seconds as it then went flying into space.

Scott now smiling, in the brief time he had been with Octavian, his confidence in that man's ability to defy the odds just kept growing.

For the first time, there seemed to be concern now that he might make it to the yellow circle. The scene animated from the table was now showing space, with the yellow portal and Octavian's shuttle heading for it. There were numbers displaying the time until he entered it.

The Mantis was communicating with two different people: both shown as animated heads projected from the table. One was installing a barrier over the yellow portal while the other was the commander of three ships ready to intervene in stopping Octavian.

To the man working on the portal's protection, it was about how long before its activation. He responded with at least eight minutes, but the field would then have to be adjusted. Anything touching it would be destroyed. The Mantis replied to him to get it ready in under five minutes.

The Commander of the ships were instructed to use a magnetic beam set at a much stronger rate than the holding dock, to secure Octavian ship in place. The mood became calm again, with the Mantis projecting a feeling of confidence.

Scott just knew it was not over, that Octavian would not give up that easily and he was right.

Credit had to be given to the commander of the three ships trying to stop Octavian. They were trying to get at least one lock on the ship. Its size being so small made it almost impossible. Like threading a needle while in a car on a bumpy road.

Scott now firmly wanting Octavian to succeed, watching him weave that small shuttle, seeing their beams missing. He was the underdog, just like when he had taken on Lord Husk. Just one man against always so many, it was hard but finally, one of the ships locked onto his shuttle. Its acceleration froze instantly, now appearing it was over.

From the shuttle appeared a much smaller craft, that was free of their holding beam set on the main shuttle. The table responded to the changes now showing a time for its arrival to the portal. The clock on the portal now showing six minutes while the smaller shuttle was showing four minutes and fifty-three seconds.

Again, the Mantis started to talk to the man working on the barrier for the yellow portal. Telling him he must work faster, that it now needs to be on in less than four minutes.

As they tried to lock onto the ridiculously small shuttle, it appeared an impossible task.

Incredibly, one of their pilots got a lock on the tiny craft, it froze quickly, everyone thinking it was over.

Then like a survivor, a hero coming out of the wreckage, Scott later said, at that moment he was so proud of Octavian. He just would not give up; he might still make it.

Octavian had put on a space suit, retrieved it from the larger shuttle, and changed into it before he used the small shuttle. Now blowing the hatch, he entered space flying headfirst towards the yellow portal.

Each second it got larger and larger, filling up his view. Finally, his fear relaxing regarding thoughts of not getting back, it would only be a couple minutes before he entered it.

The Mantis now contacted the man working on the barrier to seal the yellow hole in space. With what felt like anger he communicated it needs to be turned on at once. There were new numbers showing Octavian speed and time for his entry into the portal, it also showed his distance as it decreased till entry. It was now just under two minutes while the barrier to be ready numbers were two minutes and thirty-two seconds.

It appeared Octavian would make it; he was under one minute when he put his arms out so he would touch it that much sooner.

Three feet, two feet and then Octavian banged into the force field. His personal field charged up to a higher level sensing the greater field it now battled. The good news was that after twenty seconds he stilled lived, with his personal field never running out of power. The terrible news being he could not pass by it.

Scott was directed to a small star-ship, piloted by the young man who had initially knocked at Octavian's door. Regardless of his age, he was an expert pilot, moving the ship remarkably close to Octavian. There was an entrance that could be pressurized, which Octavian used in boarding.

Once he had taken his space suit off, he demanded to talk to the Council of Nine. What happened next Scott will never forget. Truth was he wish he had never seen it; it reminded him of Octavian speech to Lord Husk. About living long enough to do things you wish you never had done. Scott thinking you could add seeing things you wish you had never seen. Living too long, provides all those events.

Even in Scott's young life, the scene he was now seeing was horrible. Later he would say it was worse than the killings done at Lord Husk's home. Witnessing someone break down, watching them lose all their dignity, their mind and body, having a complete emotional collapse. Especially when it is someone you truly respect, was hard to watch.

Scott still clearly remembered the screams and wails of agony, Octavian had dished out, yet now hearing his cries, felt so wrong. His complete inability to to anything for his friend, just made it that much more awful.

Octavian had started by pleading with the Council to let him return, saying he would do anything they demanded to make it so. The pleading turned to begging, still the answer was no. The pilot had parked in space, hoping to return him to the yellow spot. He never looked at Octavian during his breakdown, keeping his focus on the controls and on the space beyond the window.

Scott, who was behind Octavian, saw more than the pilot. At one point, envying the pilot's lack of view. Then the crying started, at times so hard Octavian could barely see. Eventually regaining his composure and starting the process all over again.

This went on for over an hour, sixty minutes for the pilot and Scott, both who if asked would say it was the worst hour of their lives. They were both traumatized just by being near the event.

Once they had arrived back at LaTaFree, the pilot had made one big jump with full speed after that. As Octavian was leaving the ship, the young pilot looked into his eyes with his hand outstretched. Octavian who did not even look like the man who had left just a day before, returned his hand to finish the handshake.

Again, the pilot kissed his hand, then bowed saying, "It is the greatest honor in my life to have met you, Mr. Great Octavian."

There was no response from Octavian, nothing to acknowledge or discipline the gesture. He was a beaten man, a shell of his former self. Like someone in shock, more like the walking dead than a person.

At the beginning of the fourth week, Octavian's former persona started to emerge. Scott could already tell he would never be the old Octavian again. Like Lord Husk, certain events forever change who you are.

Scott was sitting in the back porch with Octavian. He wanted to know more about what had happened to him in the yellow space. Not wanting to bring him more pain that subject was not mentioned.

Octavian only had one statement about it, "I'll get back there!"

To Scott, Octavian was biding his time, making some plan that would allow his return. Maybe he had to think that, or he would go mad.

5

JOHN'S TRANSFORMATION

John Husk had finally received the meeting he was looking for, with the greatest military mind in the galaxy. Traveling only with a pilot, John had been studying Octavian's past to the point of obsession.

It is common for a hunter to become an expert on their prey, after so much studying he started to act like Octavian. Going to places by himself, where before there would be an entourage. As much as he hated him, there became an appreciation of his enemy.

With that appreciation also came power, being alone and relying only on yourself, makes you stronger. Never did he feel he had to prove something. His genius came easily in the areas he had chosen. Now it was different, only total defeat of Octavian would make things right.

Once they landed the pilot stayed with the ship, Lord John Husk was not impressed with his reception nor the building that stood before him. This meeting had cost him many leeches as payment. They had value to the men he was meeting, truly little to himself.

It was a one-story large building; the front door led into a long hallway with rooms on both sides. At the end there were double doors leading into an extremely large room, filled mostly with men, some alien life, and a few women.

On one side, was a large bar having two bartenders to cover its length. At the back was a fire pit with an old man surrounded by many other men. They were sitting in an almost completed circle.

John was led to the back where the greatest military mind was waiting.

"I have questions I want answered, they concern Octa..."

The old man interrupted him, putting his hand up to stop and spoke, "We all know who you are talking about, some names are better not spoken, they leave indexes in the UD. I am aware of what happened on your home world. What do you think caused your defeat?"

John looking down at the man replied, "I underestimated him plus he was lucky."

The old man shaking his head slowly in agreement, "You are right, but there is more."

John thinking to himself, here he was answering questions when the reverse should be happening. He was getting annoyed; being outnumbered he controlled his anger.

"I have studied him, most including myself are defeated by their greed for whatever outcome they wanted."

Now the old man's face lit up with agreement, "What do you want to know?"

"How would you defeat that man?" John was large in stature, his presence demanded respect and attention.

The old man began with, "First."

As he said that he patted his chest directly over his heart and continued, "You must get his force field, also his laser weapon, and of course what you originally wanted. Once you have these items plus two armies and total air and space control."

He stopped for a minute like he was evaluating all his words, "I give you a fifty fifty chance of succeeding. He gave the gift to your daughter, just to show you he could, while denying you. Find her, use her as bait, he does not care about her, but he has a code of honor and that might draw him to you. Once you have her, give him two weeks and if he does not appear, start sending pieces."

The old man now looking right into John's eyes said, "Are you aware of his history, he went to Pew and walked into the toughest prison in the galaxy. In less than a day it was destroyed. Before that he destroyed the First People's base on Earth which all others could not even enter. He led the Final Battle and not only repelled them but after being taken, somehow returned. And there are so many more stories, most don't live long enough around him to tell. You are lucky you still are alive, only a fool would seek that man."

This was the new John Husk, he could only hold his anger for so long, staring down at the little old man, "You are a coward."

The room had instantly changed, men stiffening, getting ready to go from friendly to killers.

The old man was unaffected and spoke, "I insulted you and you returned the favor, fair enough."

John feeling more powerful than his earlier life, here he was surrounded by strangers, standing tall, holding his own.

John spoke, "I have one last question, why did he come in the first place. He knew it was a trap yet had taken nothing from me."

The old man now started to smile, "You have not been listening." The smile turned into laughter as he finished his sentence.

"He did it for fun!" His laughter joined by all around him, except for John. As he exited the room, they were all laughing as if it was the funniest thing ever heard.

—-

"Are you ready for a space trip?" Octavian asked Scott while they were eating lunch.

"Sure, where too?" Scott answered while trying to finish his burger and fries.

"Well, I should have mentioned you can come along on one condition." Now Octavian was giving him that look, like he had revealed another secret of his friend.

"If you share your fries." Octavian had a devil's look, realizing that Scott was food eccentric and hated to share even one.

"Have one or two, now where are we going?" Scott replied, it was obvious he did not want to share even that.

Octavian call it UD, which was short for universal database. It stored most things that happened and was indexed by events and people's names. Certain things were blocked or just not recorded; an example would be trying to find a Jinn. But if you knew who had it, you could look that person up in the UD. Which would get you closer to the real prize, the Jinn.

Scott thinking how fortunate Octavian was being able to access the UD. If it were connected to everyone's chip, things would be so different. That was another thing, Scott mused, Octavian's chip was so much more advanced than everyone else, making it feel unfair.

The planet they landed on was a cross between Earth's past, when gangs ruled and modern galactic norms. Almost everyone had weapons fully displayed. Octavian was wearing a large black cape that finished with a hood the same color. On each side of the cape, he had two short swords fitted into the garment with special sleeves created.

He always wore his personal force field, which was different than what most had. Not only did it never run out of power, but Dragonfly also created the necklace the quartz crystal was held by. Most force field protectors looked like a bulky coat; Octavian's rested around his neck with the crystal on his chest. It was a great advantage he had over others that had lesser technology.

Scott was carrying a blaster, which was the standard galactic weapon. Just laser technology with electricity, still highly effective in either killing or stunning your victims. Octavian had informed him this journey might be dangerous, and it would be prudent to be armed.

Realizing that Octavian rarely listened to his own advice, having only the two short swords as weapons. He also was vague about what they were trying to do, with the response being that he just wanted to get a name.

Scott now was studying Octavian, he was walking with determination, as if he owned the streets he now was visiting. There was an aura around him, shouting contradictions. He was old but still seemed dangerous. More than that was his lack of fear, they were in a bad section of the city, yet it felt like others went out of their way to avoid him.

It was a long walk, Octavian being directed by his chip, stopped in front of a building that had been pretty in its past. Currently looking like a demolition would be in order. There were a few young men and women plus others sitting in the front, where the steps led to its door.

Scott felt they were looking for a fight or at least to command dominance over the area. Blocking most of the steps, leaving a tiny path on the right-hand side.

Octavian had not been in a good mood, since his visit to the yellow space, Scott thought. Trouble was moments away as they made their way to the door.

Octavian marched his way directly at the center of the group, stopping two steps before the young man who appeared to be the leader.

"Go Around!" That shouted at Octavian by the man sitting in front of him.

Octavian crossed both his arms then going under his cape pulled out two short swords. Leaning into the man's personal space spoke, "When I awoke this morning, I thought it is a good day to die, how bout you?"

"Your crazy, they will kill you." Was his reply

"Maybe, but I can guarantee, you will die." Octavian had spoken that without anger, which made it feel more ominous.

As Scott watched he thought, yes it looked crazy but actually Octavian had the edge. With his personal shield plus two weapons, they will not be able to shoot him. Also, knowing how fast he can move when he wants to, all that without counting that Scott also could help him.

"What do you want?" Now there was a bit of desperation from the young man, he was facing both swords. Octavian can be a scary figure, especially in a cape and hood with two weapons ready for blood.

"Tell your friends to take a walk." Octavian replied.

"Go on, walk away." Commanded the young man, with the next question from his group, where to?

Octavian spoke, "Around the block."

They still were not moving when the young man yelled, "You heard him, around the block."

As they left, he said, "Now what?"

More with a growl and lower voice than before, Octavian replied, "Get out of my way!"

With that he scuttled off, Octavian still brandishing two swords, opened the door to the building walking into the lobby.

That area had been modified into a much smaller space, fortified walls and one elevator for transportation to its upper floors. There were two benches on either side with a counter facing the door. In total there were five people not counting Octavian and Scott.

By the time Scott had entered, Octavian was at the counter leaning over, talking to the man behind it. His swords were by his sides with the men now standing up and taking notice. They all had guns but were moving in on Octavian from both sides. Appearing that they were not intimidated by his swords.

"Tell your boss that father has arrived." Octavian said.

The recipient just stared back making no actions.

Octavian now calmly spoke, "Please, I don't want to kill you all." Which still had no effect on anyone there.

As Scott watched his anger grew, no one there paid him any attention. He had pulled his gun out; it was already set to deep stun. He could tell that Octavian was in trouble or at least fighting would start momentarily.

He did not really think about it, later that aspect surprised him the most, with anger he pulled the trigger hitting one of the men closest to him.

Right after that screamed at them, "Everyone, put your hands up, high up in the air."

The next few moments seemed like everyone was in shock, maybe it was the way Scott looked, people who had never killed anyone had that look.

Scott then said, "Octavian, you can put your arms down."

Octavian slowly lowered his arms, with a half smile and continued talking to the man behind the counter.

"You see, now you got my friend upset, before everyone is dead, tell your boss that father has arrived."

Scott for his part kept moving his gun from one figure to another, he looked nervous.

Finally, contact was made with their boss who instructed the desk to send them up.

Octavian and Scott looked like the odd couple. One acting like he owned the place while the other on high alert for trouble. When the elevator stopped on the top floor they were greeted by eight men plus their leader.

All were sitting at a long rectangular table, the boss at the head, the rest stretched from him to the empty opposite end.

Octavian went to the open seat at the other end, very casually sitting down, and pulled out a cigarette. Scott had moved to a corner near his chair, wanting to stand rather than sit.

Their boss was the young man Scott had met at Octavian's home. The same man who rescued them at Lord Husk's world. It was amazing he still lived, as he was stranded there when they left him.

"Father, what do you want?"

"A name, plus at this moment, killing you for betraying me." Octavian replied.

There was an exceptionally large man sitting in the first seat below the boss who said, "Watch your mouth, old man, you could very easily leave on your back!"

Scott who could only explain that he just felt different, there was something about being around Octavian that was bringing a part of him out, he had never released before.

"If he wants to, he will kill you all."

Then a second later adding like it was obvious, "There is only eight of you."

The boss spoke first giving Octavian the man's name, and ending with, "I apologize for my friend's ignorance, please go in peace."

That enraged the man who jumped up from his chair and moved around towards his boss.

They were now facing each other as he said, "You are not worthy to lead us, I do not apologize to this old man and demand satisfaction!"

The boss was wearing a very lose fitting shirt, that had exceptionally large sleeves. With a motion that if you blinked, you missed it, he jerked his arm straight. A knife appeared from a spring-loaded devise, which he grabbed in one motion and continued its path. It landed in the throat of his enemy, which he quickly pulled out and started stabbing him in the chest area.

After much blood that splattered all over that area, the man died on the table remarkably close to his prior seat. Everyone had tensed up while the fighting occurred. It was only after that they realized Octavian had not moved a muscle, in fact he was just smoking his cigarette like nothing had occurred.

Then the boss spoke, "I had sold it to that man, he had since died. I have tried with no success to locate what you are looking for. Of course, you are more resourceful than I and may have better luck. I am sorry for my betrayal."

Octavian was unmoved and said, "Mr. Scott are work is done here." With that he moved from the chair to the door that was the elevator.

They traveled back to LaTaFree, which always felt like paradise, at least to Scott.

—-

In some ways he wanted to thank Octavian, his existence was now different, granted he still did not have the elixir of extended life, yet he was more aware of himself and surroundings. Like finding a mirror and then seeing elements you never realized you had, were John's thoughts.

The mind and body going thru a transformation, diets, and training in self defense, were just some of it. He studied battle strategies and focusing of thought. He had expanded his curiosity in old and new areas, feeling more alive than ever before.

Grudgingly, the credit was due to Octavian. The admiration regarding his enemy a byproduct of his changes. Even with that aspect, he liked the new John Husk.

Challenging himself while doing so much more alone, created personal power. Now not being afraid to get into physical conflicts, if necessary, all led to strength, confidence, and the cockiness his adversary had. As his thoughts continued the saying you become your enemy was so true.

Thinking about Octavian's actions while at his world, the old general was right, he was having fun. He secretly envied him during that time, now understanding that smile he wore, while killing his people within the circle.

Instead of just being angry in his defeat, John used it to re-imagine his total being. It only was a speed bump, a minor setback so when he does acquire it, the real John Husk will be ready. He thought about his time spent with Octavian. Things in hindsight seemed so obvious. Mr. G was right, and he should have followed his advice, instead of thinking he knew best.

Octavian would never kill himself, why could Mr. G see that so easily while it was blind to him. Asking that question to himself and answering it with the next thought. One word was all that was needed, warrior!

John Husk was a warrior; he had not known it until Octavian revealed it. Now, understanding the implications of such a thing, it is so clear that Octavian would never kill himself.

Seeing all the mistakes he made, knowing next time will be different. Currently, he was traveling alone to one of the greatest psychics in the galaxy. She also wanted leeches, which felt like nothing to him in giving. They were already sent, now he was going to get answers.

They provided a very warm greeting, leading him to a beautiful building carved into the rock bed. The mountains surrounded it, when entering, it felt like traveling to a new world. It was overly adorned with carvings, statues, and pictures. One area was a huge library holding all forms of written knowledge. There were stone carvings, scrolls, parchments, plus regular books. Another section held all types of electronic forms of wisdom.

As John was led around the structure, it was very confusing having many rooms, hallways and turns to get to where they were heading.

The room they entered was not finished having bare rock exposed, not polished or changed in anyway. There were pockets of steam rising from unseen areas. It had a humid feel with the air smelling foul.

Four women were there, two quite old, one being the person John had sought.

"Lord John Husk, I know what you are looking for, I am sad to tell, the answer will not please you."

"I am listening." John was impressed with her directness and honesty.

The old woman moved closer to him and began, "She moves from sector to sector, staying no longer than three or four days. Living deeply in the void, the biggest void in this universe. She is terrified of you and doing everything possible to not be discovered."

John listened, he was good at that, having more patience than most. His mind was sharp and analyzed the information presented.

How do you trap something that is constantly moving in the darkness? Nothing was impossible he thought, feeling more invincible than ever, a plan emerged within his mind.

"I will offer you a piece of the prize I look for, together we will find her. In those three to four days, that they rest, eventually we will be close and able to gain access. Help me and I will give you that which no other can provide." John was smart which always was helpful in persuading people to do what he desired.

The fact that she did not immediately refuse the offer, to a skilled negotiator meant it is just in the details now.

John added, "Also, I will make a large donation to your group, I have plenty of people or other assets you might need." That also was a trick to negotiations, just keep making the offer better.

Still, the old woman had not responded, John trying to think of something that would close the deal.

"I will help you to find her, also I want a sample once all has been resolved. People and money will be sent before I leave, we will go over the numbers. But I want nothing to do with your final plans, I will not help nor attend, is that agreed."

John feeling like the way Octavian thought, she was old and desperately wanted more years. That was why she agreed so readily, just the chance of more time was so compelling. He thought about his daughter, Serenity, there was admiration also for her, like Octavian, she used cunning against him.

Introspection was a virtue, which he had, with all his wealth and power. True deception when your life required it, the Lords did not have. It was a great advantage his enemies owned, which he now was going to use.

—-

They were enjoying the fireworks that LaTaFree often displayed.

Scott started their dialogue with, "When did you suspect your son betrayed you?"

Octavian sigh, "Technically he is not my son, he has a strong nature to survive. When he looked at me, I did not see a man ready to meet his end, which also was a tell."

Scott persisted, "There must have been more."

Octavian acting like he was revealing a secret, "A long time ago, I was part of a program called Reality Benders or RBs. Where certain people can modify reality mostly in small ways. That was only one aspect of that gift, which everyone has but most do not know how to gain access to it. The chip from the First People has enhanced some elements of being an RB. To put it shortly, which I have already failed to do." With that Octavian smiled and continued.

"I had a strong gut feeling he had deceived me, then checked the UD and the rest is readily apparent."

Scott going deeper into it, "And you wanted to find the Jinn to get back to the Yellow Space."

"Yes, and after a fast check of that man's life, nothing showed up. The fact that you brought back my watch and it was still there, was against all odds. Even with my long life, to have it in my possession a third time will most probably never happen."

"So, what about Lord Husk, I know you don't worry about such things, but what do you think he is doing?" Scott asked with true curiosity showing on his face.

Octavian now smiling which seemed odd considering his answer, "Definitely plotting my demise, he is smart, first he will review the past, figure out his mistakes. Then create a new situation where he cannot fail. He will have patience in setting it up, knowing that only one of us will walk away this time."

Scott having a look continued, "So what are your plans in preventing or containing it?"

Octavian's smile was so big it turned into laughter, "Can you prevent the rain or wind? It feels destined to occur. No, I have no plan, but I did not have any last time either."

That was partially correct, he made his plans while there but did have the element of surprise in multiple areas.

Scott continuing with his thoughts, maybe he had lived so long that continual existence does not have the same importance as it does to regular people. His nonchalant attitude to the real possibility of his future death was odd. Then, he remembered some conversations he had with normal old people. Most did not fear death, they lived in pain and alone during their final years.

—-

Serenity's crew were few but fully committed to their queen. Five in number, forming two women and three men. To each of them, it was a lifetime duty, protecting their queen was everything.

Many times, Serenity questioned her decisions, not even aware if what Octavian had given her even worked. There were no signs her body was any different than before she had taken it.

In her mind, if he did share his gift and she stayed around father too long, he would surely realize, which would be bad. On the other hand, she was now traveling around the great void, worried she had wasted her life on a dream and if that were not bad enough, now her father would be after her.

She had envisioned the first hundred years to go quickly and then she could enjoy the next nine hundred without worrying about her father's anger towards her.

Everything now felt wrong, between the boredom and fear, it was the worst she could imagine, and it all may be for nothing.

Octavian made it sound so simple, easy. He had wanted her to blow up the command center during the fight, to cause a distraction. She had waited until it was virtually over before having her martyrs start. Deep down she was also fearful of Octavian, if she did not do it, maybe he would have come after her too. Watching him kill all those people while smiling convinced her to fulfill her part of the deal.

Her star-ship was self sufficient, able to make food, clothing, and replacement parts. It had multiple types of power sources, some that would last well over one hundred years while others were rechargeable.

Now after months of safety, Serenity still was uneasy. Octavian had said, lose yourself in the void, its emptiness is your security. One of her followers was a technician who disabled any harm the chips inside their heads could do. He assured them they were easy to disable if you knew what you were doing.

The irony was they were close to Earth, which sits almost in the middle of the biggest void in the universe. Hiding remarkably close to where Lord John Husk ruled. They were halfway between the edge of the void and Earth's sun. Making jumps between the two as they moved across the empty blackness.

John had commissioned an extremely large star-ship having multiple shuttles plus the latest weapon systems. It also was equipped with extremely sensitive equipment for detecting other ships far away.

Having a well-trained crew plus the old woman with her psychic abilities, they started the search for Serenity. The good news was she felt they were close, compared to the size of the known universe.

It was going to be a slow process; John did not want to jump directly into wherever Serenity ship was found. Worried it would frighten her with either her ship doing another jump to escape or something even worse.

Even in the empty space of the largest void that ever existed, there were ships. That with parking their main ship far away and then only John piloting a shuttle to the target, was a terribly slow process.

John not bothered by the amount of time, he was confident that given enough focus plus luck, she would be found. The fact that he was on the path of his heart, which had long ago been forgotten, made such a difference.

A voice inside his head said it will be completed and even if it does not, you are on the right and only path to be on. That brought peace to his mind and strength to his body. His crew were well paid, having plenty of everything and like John, were happy to chase his quest.

There always was one, someone not as content as the others and remarked that it felt like the book *Moby-Dick*, John being Captain Ahab, Serenity their whale and this ship and crew on an ill-fated mission.

Time marched on, days to months, most now wanting to get back to whatever lives previously were waiting for them. John still had positive spirits and faith in his psychic. The process even at best was slow and after five incorrect targets, most were pessimistic about their future outcomes.

John's power was now at its peak, his will and determination a force that infiltrated the ship and all around him. There was already one rebellion which John personally handled. Acting like he cared and having empathy allowed the rebels to leave in a shuttle while they were near a planet.

Once the men and shuttle were on their way, John on the communicator berated the men for their lack of loyalty and weak fortitude as men. That they will never amount to anything worthy for the gift of life. Then John personally fired on the ship, it did not have a chance, exploding instantly.

Some of the crew vocalized among themselves, that it was a waste of a good shuttle.

John's thoughts were on his old teachers; examples always needed to be made.

6

REUNION

Now in his shuttle, heading at medium speed towards the eighth prospect. Knowing contact should be in less than six hours he relaxed. John knew they would check the shuttle logs, so everything had to be believable, numbers matching the story.

In his thoughts he now was on the path of Octavian, trying to model his thinking and actions towards that goal. He knew he was changing, aware that he would never again just be Lord John Husk. Once he had achieved his goals, his name must change to something sounding more grandiose. Again, thinking it should be three names like his enemy, Octavian Blanche Wright had.

As he approached the vessel in front of him, his gut feeling shouting this was the one. All the searching was the easy part, now his one and only chance was approaching. He would have to put on the best show of his life and felt ready for the task.

All the other times, either before he had sent his mayday or right after sent, responses came back. Like an unwritten rule, when a ship was in trouble other close ships would respond. The thought being, you never know when it will be you needing that type of help.

John had already sent a mayday distress call and now was quite near with no response given. Most would be upset or at least concerned about that. To John, it was a positive sign he had finally found his prey.

Becoming an actor, as we all are most of the time, he began in a desperate voice.

"Please, I desperately need supplies, please just some fuel cells, food, and water. I only have days before both run out." He was able to put fear into his voice plus the feeling of desperation. John waited but was far from done, feeling eventually he will wear them down.

"Please, please, I am extremely rich and will gladly pay you to take me to a transport station or please provide needed supplies and you will be far richer than before." This was just one aspect of his plan, knowing they did not need funds yet still offering it.

Nothing happened, no responses were seen or heard. Not even a light blinked on or off from the ship nor sound sent. John's excitement that he had found the target, fueled into his acting as he continued.

"I implore you, please if you do nothing I will die!" His voice emphasized the panic that also was shown on his face.

I have a family that needs me, wives, and children, I don't want to die, please. Look inside yourself and please show mercy. My life and the welfare of all that depend on me are begging you."

That statement had touch Serenity, she had brothers and sisters she did care about. Also, she felt bad for her father, he appeared so weak and helpless, having his death on her conscious was not part of the plan.

Her crew adamantly told her not to respond; they wanted to immediately perform a jump. Now she was in command of this ship and her life, something she had dreamed about since being a child, at least in controlling her life's actions.

This decision which ever way she decided would change her life and lives of others forever. She wondered if she was ready or really wanted to carry that type of burden till her death. If having this long life she wanted was worth the cost of people, she loved.

She did not love her father, but he had never done anything to deserve her causing his death. Then her thoughts went to Octavian, to him everything was easy. He would have no problem not responding and leaving father to die.

Against her crews concerns she got onto the communications system and responded.

"Father, I..."

"Oh my God, thank everything holy, I thought Octavian had taken you hostage or even worse. He broke my arm, gave me a compound fracture." John ended that with a chuckle.

"I was scared and then thought you might be angry with me for running away." Serenity responded thinking possibly he will not know the truth.

"Completely understandable, I could not believe the destruction that man caused. Hundreds died, and others like myself have permanently been changed. I no longer want what I had wished before. Just appreciating each day, especially with all I have is more than enough."

"Father, you are welcome aboard, I will take you wherever you wish to go."

—-

Octavian and Scott were sitting in the back porch, enjoying the night sky. Iamda, the young lady that Scott first met upon his arrival brought drinks and chips to them. Many times, Scott would bring up philosophical subjects, enjoying Octavian's unique outlook about such things.

They had been discussing the Lords and AIE on Earth when Octavian said the following.

"The Lords' time are running out; the AIE will take over once all is in place." Seeing Scott not following his logic he continued.

"Imagine placed on a big isolated undeveloped island, with a car. Now there are no roads but there are islanders. You realize they are quite stupid, so you teach them about roads. Slowly they developed roads which makes their lives easier. Then you convinced them that if they had roads to every major spot on their island, life would be even better. Finally, they have roads to every major and minor parts of their world. It is then that you eradicate all the people there. Their only purpose to create the infrastructure you needed without you having to do it. That is what the AIE are doing with the Lords. Soon their purpose will be completed and not needed, then they will be eliminated."

Scott looking at him, Octavian seemed so sure of all he spoke.

"When will that happen?" Scott asked.

"Soon." Was his response, with a very indifferent attitude to the affair. Then sensing his friend's discomfort with his words added the following.

"I used to think in terms of good and evil, they are just perspectives. Yes, I live by a moral code, but it is just rules that I have agreed to live by. Whether they are really good or bad are defined by just me. Imagine two dogs, one a rescue dog for lost people and the other a police dog to get criminals. Neither are good or bad, if anything in my way of thinking both are wrong to have."

Scott now looking directly into his friend's eyes asked, "How could the rescue dog be bad, it is saving people's lives."

Octavian stared back and answered, "You are changing its harmony for your purpose, negating it to never achieve its own perfection."

Scott had brought up in the past that with Octavian's help, the people of Earth could regain their freedom and planet. Octavian's answer was short and to the point, never. Still Scott held hope that one day he would change his mind.

Octavian's health had been failing lately, in the mornings he would throw up and by evenings the headaches came. Currently, he was looking pale when Scott asked him if he was okay, his answer was the following.

"Maybe Dragonfly's potion is wearing off, or the mixture I made was not quite right."

Scott asked, "Are you going to see a doctor?"

Octavian laughing replied, "Only people wanting to live go to doctors."

Scott looking at him with a hard stare, "And you don't want to live?"

Octavian with his patented smirk, "Not enough to see a doctor."

—-

The psychic was adamant on her position; Lord Husk was good; they needed to let him have time to carry out his mission. The captain of John's star-ship wanted to move in closer to Serenity' ship. Worried that Lord Husk might need backup or worse, possibly injured or dead.

"You will ruin everything, patience, and faith, is all that is needed." The old psychic said as she gave him a look.

The captain gave up quickly, he could always show it was her advice that kept him from helping.

John was allowed to dock and enter the ship, he was brilliant in speech and manner making all, but two members trust his good intentions. Having the ability to express one's thoughts eloquently was a tremendous gift.

He told them the experience with Octavian had changed his life, made him appreciate so many tiny things, the blessings that are always around him. That he had received something better than extended time, gratitude for the life he had.

John could be very convincing, especially since Serenity wanted to believe his words. How great it was all turning out, she had extended life, and her father now, a better man than before. Deep down, she was still having trouble totally believing him. Her thoughts trying so hard, saying people have near death experiences that change them.

"Let's return to our planet and have a royal party, the type that has never been seen before. To celebrate new beginnings while never forgetting how blessed we are." John wanted them to return to Husk planet and was pitching the idea.

"How about we all sleep on it and tomorrow you can give me your answer. If not, then please take me to a transfer station." John ended that with a beautiful smile. He had changed into a slimmer and more muscular image than before. Also, he had the ability to soften his voice and fix his big eyes on his listeners, making it hard to deny his requests.

John was slipping out of sanity; he realized the change he was feeling yet described it with a different word. To him it could not be verbalized in just one word. It was a new type of freedom, where there were no rules. He could do whatever impulses came, with no restrictions.

He thought about Octavian and all the people he killed, after killing so many and always walking away, that was freedom. Caring nothing about society's values, just doing what you want. Better than that, it gives you power, makes you stronger and most importantly, extremely dangerous.

To succeed on the path of Octavian, he had to let his inhibitions go. Freedom was just a word, truly living it means there were no rules. He would show them that tomorrow, just another step till his final goal reached.

Thinking of the Shakespeare play *As You Like It* the lines "All the world's a stage, And all the men and women merely players." His best performance, that was what it was to John. Nothing really mattered, it was a show, and he needed to be more than just a lord. He wanted to be legendary.

They all met in the kitchen; it had a table that could seat eight people. Given the few people aboard it was natural to gather there. John was in Octavian mode, searching for weapons and creating a plan on the go.

He was aware there were five of them not counting Serenity. Currently four were at the table plus his daughter.

It had a long rectangular shape with a small space at one end between it and the wall. The other side had a wide-open area that formed the rest of the kitchen. Serenity was at the head of the table, the side closest to the wall, with two men sitting on either side below her.

John sat two people away from Serenity which provided her as much protection from him as possible.

Once the food was served, John began his attack. He stood up with some food stuck on his fork and said the following.

"I have eaten in establishments thru out the galaxy, from the Blue Winds on the Orion's planet Zefron to the gourmet gardens of Adela. Never have I tasted food such as this." He was moving towards the head of the table where Serenity sat. Traveling on the inside wall where there was little room for any movement. He continued to rave about how wonderful the food was.

"Never have I tasted anything that compares to what I now have before me." As he was raving about the quality and taste of the meal, his arm with the fork was also waving around. When he was within arms distance of Serenity, her guard quickly rose providing a wall between the two. His stare at John said I am not scared of you; he also was a large man who looked unmovable.

John made sure his active arm with the fork was above both arms of the man confronting him. Instead of returning his stare, John half turned like he was accepting the impasse.

He began speaking, "It is not just the ingredients, no it must have been the process of..."

At that moment, John who was watching the man between his daughter and himself, thru his peripheral sight saw opportunity and without thoughts or hesitation, committed all his focus on action.

His arm laterally moved with extreme force, stabbing the man standing, in his left eye. It embedded itself in that socket, sticking out looking like an obscene image of a mad artist. At the same exact moment, he screamed in pain sounding like agony crying, John grabbed his weapon and shot the other man sitting across from him.

Then without any wasted action while turning again to face his first victim, he fired his weapon the second time. Now John had grabbed Serenity's hair moving behind her facing the next two opponents.

One woman was unarmed and much less threat than the other. Using Serenity as a shield he fired the third time, killing her as she had her weapon pointed at him. Her hesitation in either killing someone or hurting Serenity was her downfall.

The entire event happened so quickly that the two survivors were still taking it all in. Unlike John, who had a plan and with the advantage of surprising them, was moving on to its next stage.

"Duct Tape!" Shouted John, "I know its here, you get it now!" As he was looking at the woman in front of him. She went to a shelf in the other corner of the room and opened the first drawer, pulling out a thick roll of gray tape two inches wide.

"Bring it to me now." John commanded, as the smile on his face grew larger. Grabbing it from her he forced Serenity's arms behind her body while rolling the tape around her wrists and then hands. Once finished she was not getting free quickly, John then re-grabbed her hair with one hand while the gun was in his other.

Without warning in cold blood, John shot the woman who had just helped him. Pulling his daughter by the hair he rushed out of the room, heading for the command center.

He was thinking about Octavian's luck, to him it now was not luck at all. John also was getting lucky but using that word was wrong. His mind explained it as the universe enjoys players, people that provide a show and in gratitude it gives them an edge. Like a reward for making things interesting, its attention tips the scales more in that players favor.

His mind raged or maybe it was just personal power that as you do more daring things they collect up and then provides benefits in the form that people call luck. Whatever the definition he was getting luckier in all things, yet to him it was not a gift but an earned benefit.

The last person alive was a loner, who had argued someone should always be in the command center. His logic was correct, but execution cannot be ignored, which he had not cared about.

He was listening to music streamed directly within his head while also playing his favorite game. All his attention on personal actions not checking any controls or indicators. In truth, he just did not want to be around Lord John Husk, being a loner in general.

John entered the room with Serenity in front of him, using her as a shield. Recognizing his enemy was distracted without any warning, he shot him in the back. Then using the rest of the duct tape, he secured Serenity onto one of the chairs in the command center. Moving the dead man from the room, he occupied a seat next to Serenity and set the course to his original ship.

She had been passive the entire time, now she spoke.

"Father, this is not like you, I fear you are going insane." It was spoken with a caring tone.

John smiling, feeling great as he answered, "Probably, it is a wonderful form of freedom. Just remember, this insane man just had taken over your ship, killed your crew, and you now are my prisoner, not bad for crazy." Laughing as he observed his first daughter.

"Why are you doing this, in this way?" Serenity wanted to get her former father back, trying to understand why he was behaving in the way he was.

John who was euphoric responded, "I am on the path of Octavian." Like that would answer all her inquiries.

Serenity replied, "He would never kill those people like that, he believes in a sporting chance."

Now John's emotions changed to a touch of anger mixed with scorn, "I watched him firsthand, he killed men while they begged for mercy, his smile never left his face. I will kill him but first strip him of his personal shield, get the elixir of extended life, and have his laser weapon."

Serenity always knew her father's quest for power yet now she felt scared.

"What is my role to play in all this?" She asked, looking into her father's eyes.

John replied, "Now you are disappointing me, I am making the perfect trap, you are the bait."

They arrived back at his former ship; John greeted with a hero's welcome. Many were extremely impressed that Lord Husk on his own, had accomplished all he had done. The psychic demanded to be returned home, which John obliged. His crew had formed great admiration for their leader; John set out to find something impossible. Not only did he find and conquered it, now was much closer to the final prize, it was impressive.

7

TROUBLE AHEAD

After dinner it was typical for Scott and Octavian to go to the back porch and talk.

Octavian began, "I have to leave here, can't afford the rent." With that chuckling to himself.

Scott first assumed he was joking, yet his inner instinct was saying Octavian was serious about leaving. Then he thought, in all the time around Octavian, he never asked for any money from him. Between the ship rides, plus the expensive cost of living in LaTaFree, it all adds up.

Octavian continued, "I did not mention that to John, as I felt he would not consider it an issue, I had many fortunes, they eventually run out if you live long enough." Again, his smile turned to laughter then finished into a sad look.

Scott asked, "Why don't you sell or market one of your inventions?"

Octavian went into a rant on the word inventions.

"No one invents anything, everything is already there, it should be referred to as discovered and most of the time it is just rediscovered. Take Dragonfly, most would say she created time-crystals, when what she did is rearrange the electrons and protons into a better position where they then continually react to each other in a way that is very productive. My point is she did not create the electrons, protons, or crystals; they were waiting for their discovery. They are not my creations, and with all new things, some will benefit, most will not.

Now your book writing I like, to me that is as close to creation as you can get. And its sales are strictly a voluntary choice of the reader. No one is forced to buy or read it, did you know I had authored a few books. I did not sell many, but you are a better writer than I."

Scott taking it all in, "Well maybe my book will sell well, the profits will be divided between us. And then we can come back to live here."

Octavian with a smile said, "Good luck with that."

Scott then asked where they would be going with Octavian responding.

"It's time for me to go back to space, I have lived decades out there. No more planetary rules and expenses. I found an old ship which has a good reputation of staying in the sky. Also, I can afford to pay it in full." With that Octavian just kept smoking and staring into the night.

Scott thought about Iamda, the woman of their home, of course she would be going with Octavian. They would tease each other constantly but when it mattered, she would always follow his lead. She had left her husband without looking back when they had escaped Lord Husk's domain.

Octavian started speaking, "Of course, Mr. Scott, you are welcome to come or move on with your life. Being around me can be dangerous," now chuckling.

Scott replied, "When will we be leaving?"

"Soon," Octavian answered.

Many times, trouble comes on the most beautiful days when old problems are finally forgotten, and life appears to have moved on. Those thoughts were in Scott's mind as he now was dealing with the knock at the door.

His instincts had become stronger, which he attributed to being around Octavian. At the door was a young woman, standing without a smile waiting for an answer to her knocking. Scott had a strong instinct to tell her to go away, as Iamda had told him.

Octavian was in his study working on his own book, he really was like clockwork in his daily life. He would loudly state that the invisible hands of time do not control him, yet without a watch he appeared to never stray from their decisions.

Scott was at the door, which he opened and stepped outside to greet this new visitor. His rational mind saying why do you assume this will bring trouble, a flaw Octavian had commented on, how common people's thoughts about the unknown always think doom and destruction await.

Once outside their conversation began, Scott spoke first.

"What can I do for you?"

The woman was young in her early twenties, little in size yet having a strong spirit. She looked smart and tough, someone who would not compromise on whatever she was after.

"I need to talk to him." Spoken like a task she did not want to perform.

Scott trying to be patient, "Exactly who are you looking for."

"You know who, you were at this door just like I am here now, I only need to give him a message."

Scott who could be stern with his face, words, and actions.

"Give me the message!" He was blocking the entrance, his countenance implied no one will enter this home without my approval.

"I have to do it, all I will say, a life is on the line, maybe many lives, once I give him the message I will be gone."

Octavian now made an appearance, standing within the door frame inside his home and spoke.

"Mr. Scott, please invite our guest in so we can both hear this message that is so important. In fact, I had been expecting someone just like you, would be arriving here. Please take her to the back porch and I will be there shortly."

After a few minutes Octavian entered the back porch taking his usual seat. There were two seats and a bench that was across from them. Scott had taken the other seat that was next to Octavian, both now situated and ready to hear the message.

"Lord Husk demands you come to Husk's world within two weeks. If you do not, he will send you pieces of Serenity. Also, he demands that you provide the same elixir you had promised before your betrayal. In addition to that your personal shield must be relinquish and a working laser stick device that has an on-off switch be given. What is your response to his demands. And for the record, you killed my father."

Octavian had a hard stare while he answered, "For the record, I am not sorry about your father, I hope he died with honor and was not one of the beggars pleading for mercy."

That was more than she could withstand, "He was a good man!"

You know who I feel sorry for." Now he waited just looking at the young lady and then continued.

"You, your father, and John plus everyone else who are around now, only because of the warriors at the Final Battle, the only heroes I know. People who gave up everything to protect others they did not even know. The warriors at the Final Battle, they I feel sorry about. You see, living or dying means nothing."

Again, he waited, making the next statement that much more powerful.

"Being on the right side is everything. Yes, I have a lot of blood on my hands, including your father's, don't kid yourself, blood is now on your hands too. John has gone insane, and you think I should care about Serenity? She and I made a deal, we both lived up to the bargain, what makes you think I owe her something?"

Scott had not said a single word, just watching with his intense way, eyes fixed on the target, ears listening to each sound made. He was surprised how Octavian was handling the situation, yet he was correct in not having any responsibility for Serenity, she had made her choices.

The woman asked, "What makes you think you are always on the right side and why would you suggest Lord Husk is insane?"

Octavian was intense with all his actions and words currently, more animated with his hands and body movements.

"No father would cut up his daughter for just the possibility of getting someone's attention. He has moved well past the line of sanity. People that oppose me are always on the wrong side, the list of bodies proves that."

Now the young woman regained her mission goals with the next question.

"Are you coming and do you accept the stipulations or not?"

Scott thinking now we are at the meat of the matter, the current silence deafening.

"I will come within two weeks…"

Scott interrupted Octavian, saying, "We will be coming!" Then looked back at his friend to continue.

Octavian talking directly to Scott, "Are you sure, I believe this is a one-way ticket." From the look Scott returned he continued now talking to the young woman in front of him.

"We will be coming, I will bring the elixir, give my personal body shield up and."

At that point Octavian started to laugh which upset the woman.

"You think this is funny?" She asked looking at him in disbelief.

Octavian who still was chuckling responded.

"Tell John, I left that there on purpose to see if he was smart enough to make it work, obviously he was not up to the task. I will give you a secret, quartz crystals have special properties." Now again he stopped to create a dramatic effect.

"They are alive, he should try talking to it. Yes, I will bring one with an on-off switch. All I ask from John is that he lets Mr. Scott and Serenity, live and leave after it is over."

For the first time she smiled, which was an incredibly beautiful version of her face.

"Goodbye." Then she waited a moment to create her own effect and added, "I will see you there."

Once she had left, it felt surreal to Scott, everything was the same and yet now felt different. Octavian had not changed in anyway, acting like the meeting meant nothing.

Scott began, "So what is your plan?"

"Don't have one, the last time I had the surprise factor plus John underestimated me, and I barely survived. This time neither of those elements will be present." Octavian did not appear worried or concerned.

Scott then suggested, "Well you know so many people, why not get some help?"

Octavian for the first time showed emotion, which was anger, "No, this is not that important, too many have already paid when I had called for their help. The people that showed up for the Final Battle all answered that call. I did not have that choice, yet I wonder if I would have if I did. I believe I would, but it will never be known.

They all made the decision, just like you now, made the decision to come with me. I knew this would be coming. Who wants to live a life always looking over your shoulder.

John is turning into me, killing his daughter slowly, shows his focus and determination. If nothing else, it affects your enemy. I have a long history with many actions I regret, that I am ashamed of.

If the threat of killing Serenity failed, he would just try something else. This cannot be avoided."

Scott now somber asked, "But we have a chance, right?"

Octavian had that sly look, it could be compared to the cat that ate the canary smile.

"There is a very slim, almost impossible incredibly improbable chance."

John was euphoric, lately his personal power was showing itself all the time, at least that was the way if felt to him. The trap was almost ready, hearing news that Octavian was coming within two weeks would complete everything.

He knew it would be the fourteenth day that Octavian would arrive. Things like that he now had great intuition about. John felt connected to the universe, a true one on one relationship. He was given extra knowledge about upcoming futures. Confidence to handle any actions personally, he truly could not put it into words what it was.

John related it to his personal power, as each accomplishment gave him more strength to carry out even bigger goals.

His planning and focus now paying off, after Octavian left the first time, he felt all was lost. Now, not only will he have even more than before, but he also truly earned it. His thoughts went to Octavian, who lived freely in his mind. Once he understood who he was dealing with, defeating him would not be that hard. John thinking he now understood Octavian, that man really was looking for death. It just had to be presented in the proper way.

John did miss Mr. G, people like Lord John Husk, have few friends if any. They had a special connection that happens when both have mutual respect for each other. He remembered clearly how Octavian had killed him, without respect or honor. John would avenge that, Mr. G deserved a better death.

Before Octavian, those types of thoughts never entered into John's mind. Once the past events were replayed within his brain, realizing secrets that now were obvious. Even in the way Octavian had killed his friend.

He started a birth program understanding that trading his leeches with others in the galaxy had value. The irony, it was cheap to do yet so many races were willing to give much to have them.

John's vision of grandeur had grown as his personal power became greater each day. Very shortly his transformation from Lord to God was coming. So many new achievements waiting for a man like himself.

The greatest gift Octavian had given him was having no fear. With that, people go so much further than they could possibly imagine. He had fought and survived against Octavian; he was special where others were weak.

John decided to have the event outside like the first time, yet during the daylight hours, on a beautiful day. He had a canopy setup over his royal throne with streamers spreading in a radial pattern. They had roses and other types of flowers weaved into the ropes creating a magical look.

It was setup down by the lake, which on its own was a beautiful peaceful area. Once the path ended the lake appeared, its edges following an invisible curve that continued along its entire length.

There were three walls with ledges to sit on and enjoy the water. They were deployed around the lake in three different areas with the last area open to the pathway.

Behind them were large bushes that blocked the view behind while giving the appearance of the walls having a backrest. Beyond all that was open land that flowed with hills, trees, and grasslands.

Once off the pathway and heading to the right in front of the first of three short walls, was where Lord John Husk had setup his personal area. To the right of that were two cages, having bars that crisscrossed their design.

Height, length, and width all being the same in size, creating a nine-foot square prison. Serenity occupied one cage while the other was empty for now.

Even though there was plenty of space, there also were plenty of people. Beside the army of soldiers at the back of the lake and then a different army around Lord Husk, there were many others.

The people who had traveled with Lord Husk in finding Serenity, were impressed with his abilities were also there. Then there were the musicians, that only could be described as an orchestra with a chorus. Of course, a documentary crew, to capture all the action so Lord Husk can use for his later enjoyment.

That day was special in so many ways, the weather put on its most beautiful smile, providing perfect warm temperatures without being hot. A cooler gust of wind occasionally passed by.

There was no set time for his arrival, a message was sent that they were on their way, now just a matter of waiting. Music could be heard; it had a festive atmosphere.

In contrast there were two prison cages with one already occupied. Making it feel like an odd entity that was out of place, having no right to be there.

Octavian looked at Scott, "Are you ready for this? It is not too late to change your mind. Keep your hands at chest level and wait till you feel it is too late, then wait another minute. Your mind will control everything, good luck." With that Octavian was extremely relaxed considering what was coming.

Scott was just the opposite, hyped up, the gloves he wore were very tight while the suit under his clothes also felt stiff. This was going to be a first in many ways, so much unknown awaiting.

His thoughts went to his friend, just in their brief time together he witnessed many different sides of his character. Now he felt Octavian had miscalculated, his plan poorly thought out, with many faults eager to bring failure.

Sitting next to him, yawning like he was going home after a long day. This very well could be his last space flight. As he looked at him again, Octavian was sleeping.

Time always moves quickly when trouble is approaching, thought Scott. Within less than an hour they would be at Husk's world. The first time he traveled there, he was so excited about meeting Lord Husk.

Feeling naïve then, having changed so much, yet there were similarities too. Both times not knowing what the outcome would bring. For the first time he contemplated Octavian meeting his end. Being near him, lures one into a false sense he will always be around.

Octavian was walking into the lion's den, unarmed, against many. As Scott's mind continued, yes, he has done that before. Yet this time, he would be without his personal force-field, vulnerable to any weapon that finds him.

Scott did not like his plan, in his mind with a little modification they might have had a chance. Octavian would not budge, and now they were almost there. Two against hundreds, a wave of depression fell on Scott's spirits.

Just then, Octavian was wide awake, there was an eager tone to his voice as he asked, "How long before we arrive?"

Scott replied, "About fifteen minutes, you sound eager to be there."

Octavian looking into his eyes, "There are few moments as big as death, we will all die, how we died and what we have done, are what matters. Many deaths are worst then what I face now. It still is not too late to change your mind."

If depression had occupied Scott's spirits before, now the warrior came out.

"It's going to be glorious." With that, he smiled back at Octavian.

After landing and leaving the shuttle, they were greeted like foreign dignitaries and led down the path to the lake.

Music was playing with banners and streamers all about, it had a party atmosphere. That changed quickly once they arrived at their designated spots. Scott was taken to the second empty cage, now both had occupants.

Octavian was led to a spot that was thirty feet from John's throne. The second army on the opposite side of his location could not be seen. That because there were so many people, soldiers, personal guards, shipmates from John capturing Serenity and the first army, spread out and around Octavian.

Scott was next to Serenity, which was the good news, unfortunately people blocked his view of Octavian, even though he was not that far away from him. He caught glimpses every now and then but could hear clearly all that was happening.

When John rose from his seat the music stopped with the sounds of nature finally coming thru.

"Thank you, Mr. Octavian Blanche Wright, for your appearance. Before we begin, I want your personal force-field."

Then after a couple of seconds added, "Please." John was being nice, which he could do easily.

Without speaking, Octavian removed his necklace with the blue crystal and handed it to the man who was in front of him. Once John had it in his possession, he put it on another man and shot him. Then commanded many to shoot him. After it was proven to be genuine, John put it around his neck.

Instantly John felt its power, giving the wearer the feeling of invulnerability. That type of power with the right man, can do things others can only dream about. John's thoughts flooded his body, ready to take the next step in becoming a God.

"Now I want the elixir." John already was becoming more powerful, less caring about politeness.

Without words, Octavian put his hand inside his shirt to a hidden pocket on the inside and pulled out a bottle that had a whitish liquid. Handing it to the same man who had taken his pendant.

Again, it was brought to Lord Husk who without hesitation opened the glass bottle and drank the liquid.

John just knew it was authentic, he now had extended life, hundreds of more years. He had put his mind to it, yes there were setbacks but now he had what very few others would ever experience. Each item getting him closer to the eventual goal, killing Octavian. It was all going too perfectly.

"Now give me your light-stick!" John commanded, all subtlety gone. The power of his new personal shield flooded his mind about his invincibility.

Octavian passed it to another man, who ran it to Lord Husk. Once he held it and examined it for a minute, a three-inch circular laser beam lit the ground. John now had an on-off switch. He had everything he initially wanted from Octavian, even more than he imagined. That bar had now moved; John was not done.

"Now take everything else that is left, including his clothes." John said with a laugh.

Octavian started to give the man in front of him what last possessions he had. Then he removed his shoes and socks, shirt, and pants.

"All your clothes!" John was feeling his personal power growing with each of his demands.

Octavian removed his underwear, standing the way he was born, bare to the world.

So many scars, wounds that had healed yet left their mark. Burns with the skin never reverting to its original form. Surgeries showing controlled stitches, whippings that never healed correctly. His right android arm secured onto his bones with micro bolts.

They were not just on his arms or back but everywhere. His chest and legs, from thighs to feet. His buttocks plus even his private area, all had wounds.

To the music performers plus others who were not soldiers, their faces showed the horror of what his body displayed.

Yet the soldiers saw something different, respect. Each wound meant he had survived some battle. They were like medals, badges of honor. The more someone had the greater the respect they deserved. The man in front of them had more then any had ever seen.

"Secure his arms!" Shouted Lord John Husk, as he now rose from his throne. Two large men each grabbed one of Octavian's arms. As John approached, he was wearing a large leg guard that rose above his knees. It had spikes just waiting to make contact with anything.

John speaking as he approached, "Here is Octavian, but that is not your real name, the great Plutoneus stands naked and defeated before me. And it was not even hard to do. I have spoken with people afraid to mention your name, they were fools. Your life will end whenever I decide. Before that happens, I want to leave you something to remember me by."

With that John displayed a long curve knife, that looked extremely sharp. He moved the blade in the sunlight, causing a blinking of light if they met anyone's eyes.

Octavian had not spoken; his eyes locked on John. A transfer of power, one man now had nothing while the other everything. Not just in possessions but also in spirit. Broken and waiting for the inevitable end while John looked like he had finally been crowned the victor.

No music was heard, nor sounds from all the spectators and soldiers, even nature was quiet, waiting for this moment to have its time.

"Even if your time is short, I want you to remember who did this to you." John ended that with the point of his knife. He started on the right side of Octavian's chest. It was a straight line starting an inch from his chest's nipple going downward in a straight line to his navel. At the end he curved the bottom to make a J.

Octavian's blood was running down his chest and working its way to the ground. He had not uttered a sound nor made any move to resist. Now John started to work on the other side of his chest.

Two lines heading down with a third making the trip across Octavian's chest, on the left side. They formed a crude H, now he was marked to never forget John Husk.

The two men were staring at each other, John ready to plunge the knife into Octavian's heart. There is a look in the eyes that is a tell, still no words were spoken.

Scott was trying to see, there just were too many people. Mostly soldiers but also others, it was the look on some faces, even soldiers that really concerned him. He was waiting for a signal, a yell from Octavian, something to tell him to start now.

Octavian told him he would know when, now he could take it no longer. Observing a man's face grimace at what he was seeing, to Scott it was the sign.

Turning to Serenity he commanded, "Lay face down, now!"

The guards watching their cages started to pay attention to Scott.

Putting his hands up to his shoulder, and with the thought to destroy his cage, the first thing that happened was too fast for anyone to see. His gloves turned into fragments of their former form.

Ten crystals, each a separate ring, one on each finger plus thumbs, Scott's time had come and the warrior that lived inside him released. Each crystal worked individually but also as one in obtaining their goal. The laser beams were varied sizes, sometimes crisscrossing their paths.

They destroyed his cage while also making sure no part of it touched Scott's body. It was so dramatic it attracted everyone's attention, even John stopped just before he was about to kill Octavian.

Instantly the soldiers and even John's attention went to the current threat. They were shooting Scott, but his body armor just would not fail. At the same time his finger's lasers were killing everyone around him.

Ty was a soldier; it was his family's heritage. His great grandfather had started the tradition, and it lasted for each generation after. He had answered the call, went to the Final Battle, and died protecting the galaxy. Ty's family never forgot that war and the stories that went with it. Never believing he would ever see Plutoneus, to his family he was a legend, bigger than life itself, the reason they had all chose their current path.

It was killing him watching what was happening, thinking to himself that he was moments from throwing his whole career away. He had setup two smoke bombs with his fingers clutching the trigger. As soon as the distraction happened, instead of looking into it, he pulled the trigger.

The goggles he was wearing allowed him to see heat signatures, both smoke bombs landed in perfect spots. Within seconds that area was invisible to the naked eye.

Ty was big and strong; he had a wonderful smile when he let it out. Now he was all business, running right into the densest area of smoke. Octavian was there in the smoke, looking confused, trying to find a weapon. He was on his knees crawling around when Ty found him.

"I am a friend." Ty said as he approached. By this time, many people were shooting, not sure what was happening.

Scott was so deadly most were now avoiding him. John had decided he would have to stop Scott as the others could not even get close. He figured his laser weapon was stronger and it might have a chance.

Serenity was in disbelief; Scott had turned into an unstoppable force. When he looked back at her, with one hand pointed towards her cage and the other in front of him, five laser beams destroyed her prison.

She ran directly to him, wrapping her arms around his stomach as she clung to his back.

"Go back up the path, there's a ship waiting for us." Serenity said excitingly into his ear.

Every time John had a clear view and had taken a shot, someone would crisscross the path blocking his view and weapon's energy beam. He had killed many trying to get to Scott, who now was moving away from John.

To John, he was running away moving up the path that led from the lake to the main home. Soldiers were shooting back at John, and others. As John was killing people randomly, still trying to get a clear path to shoot Scott, he was causing pure chaos.

Also, there were so many people, just trying to move away from Scott made it difficult. By the time he had a view again, Scott was gone. More smoke grenades were being deployed by others, with soldiers shooting in all directions.

As Scott and Serenity moved up the path, there was an overgrown trail leading to the right.

"Take that path!" Serenity shouted with excitement.

Scott's adrenaline was pumping as he trampled the brush below his feet. It had taken a slight arc to the right which opened to a clearing.

There a shuttle was waiting, with two people outside waving to come quickly towards them.

"Come with me, I will show you a life you can't imagine. There is only death back there, Octavian has died, please there is nothing left back there for you." Serenity pleaded with Scott, who was now her savior.

Scott's mind went to Octavian's speech about not if you live or die but how you lived and died that mattered.

"If he is dead, I will avenge him, I need his clothes." As Scott pointed to one of the men standing there.

Scott then added, "Time for you to go." After changing into the man's clothes which was a standard outfit worn by most Lord Husk's personnel.

Ty ran out to Octavian who was on his knees moving slowly towards the side Ty had came from.

"I am a friend." Was Ty's first words then added, "Coming to help."

He grabbed Octavian's arm and pulled him towards where he had left his supplies. There were backpacks laying around, Ty opened one and pulled out a yellow poncho. Its purpose was for the wearer to be located, the bright yellow and shiny material shouted to be seen.

Knowing that was the worst thing to put on Octavian while also feeling they had truly little time to get away, he said, "Wear this."

Octavian had not spoken till then, after putting the poncho on he said, "I need a knife."

Ty instinctively gave him his knife which Octavian did not like.

"No, that's too small. Need a bigger one." Ty looked at him, the man still wanted to fight, he was not looking to escape. Going thru a different backpack he pulled out a fifteen-inch knife with a slight curve where the tip ended.

Octavian did not speak but smiled taking the weapon. The smoke was disappearing only having small areas it now covered. He now stood up and was ready to go back when Ty interrupted.

"What are you plans, where are you going? Rub this cream on your chest, it will help the wounds and kill the pain. You don't have a personal shield. Let me help you."

Octavian looked at the man who was trying to help him, "I am going to the wall, not feeling pain and a shield won't stop the weapon I gave John."

Ty then offered to put a smoke screen around the wall and help him get to wherever he was going to. After multiple shots near the wall which now was invisible to the naked eye, they made their way there.

The goggles Ty had allowed him to see the outlines of objects making it relatively easy to get there. Once they approached Octavian slowed down, like he was searching for the perfect spot. Ty was trying to block him from any shots fired that might find him. It felt like they were crawling forward when finally, Octavian said the following.

"Push me between the wall and the bushes and then leave." As he said that he laid down horizontally on the wall, moving his left hand to push him down. It was harder than Ty thought it would be. The bushes were firm with little thorns extending from them. When Ty finished, Octavian had disappeared. He slowly walked back to where he had started from, looking at the wall which was now becoming clear as the wind was moving the smoke quickly away.

The sky had darkened with a storm itching to show itself.

Scott had put on a second set of gloves, which Octavian had recommended he bring. Putting his head down and wearing a cap he reentered the lake area. The soldiers had stopped shooting and were retrieving their lost comrades. The generals were tallying the bill for each life lost while others were searching the grounds for Scott, Serenity, and Octavian.

John was surrounded by his people who had suggested that Octavian must have died or crawled away. Either way it was a victory, they said maybe someone had taken the body as a souvenir. Getting frustrated with what he perceived their stupidity; he ordered them all to go away. John now enjoyed being on his own, his power now was at its highest. He needed no one to occupy his space.

John put himself in his enemy's mind, where would I go, knowing I am wounded and defenseless. As he thought and kept looking at the ground his eyes followed ahead. There by the wall was the last of the smoke fading. Why deploy smoke by the wall, were his thoughts.

That led him to walk towards the wall where the smoke lingered. His thoughts were he had won, now having extended years plus the best personal shield in the universe. Not only that but a weapon that could kill anything. His spirit was feeling wonderful, powerful, the universe was waiting for his commands.

He was at the middle wall which was directly opposite the path that led to the lake. He saw both armies getting ready to leave. The two cages destroyed with his people waiting at his throne. The weather had now darkened with winds gusting in both directions. Like nature could feel John's power and was acknowledging it.

"I, Lord John Megatron Husk, have defeated the Great Plutoneus with my own hands. I have his personal shield and weapon. No one can stop me!" He paused as he was shouting and looked at the crowd around him. John was feeling all powerful, the energy within his body had no limits.

He wanted to yell again so he began, "Do you all hear me, no one, and I mean no one, can stop me anymore!" As he was yelling, he noticed their faces changing, thinking it was what he was saying and yet, it felt like something more.

As John was yelling the second time, like a yellow sun rising behind him, there from nowhere to on the wall was Octavian. John who was so into his speech and connecting with his audience, saw and heard nothing that was happening behind him.

When he finished his last word there was one word coming from behind and to the right of him. As he turned around, for he had clearly heard that word addressed to him.

"Wrong!" Octavian shouted as he leaped off the wall towards John. Catching John by surprise his knife hit him on the chest while also knocking him over with his laser stick falling from his hand, with John landing on his back and Octavian on his chest.

The knife had a sharp point yet was unable to penetrate John's under garment. He was wearing his own body armor plus a personal shield combo, besides now also having Octavian's pendant shield.

The body armor was doing its job, no matter how hard Octavian pushed it would go no further. John had lost his advantage of size and strength being on his back. He was holding the knife from him with his hands on Octavian's arms, pushing in the opposite direction.

At the same moment, they both realized Octavian would not be able to kill him. That gave John the ability to remove his right arm from stopping the knife and smash Octavian on his left side, pushing him somewhat off and they both now were turned.

John's right side slightly off the ground while Octavian's right side had met the dirt below. With the change of position, the knife had moved off John's chest but was now pointed at his neck.

Again, both realized the change and pressed for the advantage. Octavian had beat him by a second and was pushing the knife right for John's throat.

In John's mind the situation had worsened. Now he had to deal with the knife which could easily cut his neck and was close to accomplishing its mission. Still, most of his power was unable to help him. Now his arms had to stop the threat, and any loss of focus could be disastrous.

Octavian's smile now bigger, there was blood lust in his eyes, new power coming to his body from the anticipation of victory. The knife kept moving closer, it was millimeters from touching John's throat.

For the first time, John realized how precarious his current situation was. He might actually die, that thought had never entered his mind, until now. Octavian was in his head, knowing there would be a surge of strength when his victim realized his death was close.

Octavian had never taken his eyes off John's eyes. He saw the panic happen and was ready. Knowing he could not lose his advantage, Octavian equalize the last of John's resistance with his own in a push. It cut into John's neck and then sunk deeply within.

As John was trying to talk, mostly blood coming down his chin, pleading with his eyes to let him live.

Octavian turned his wrist making the injury horrific, then moved its across John's throat, leaving a cut that could never heal. John died shortly afterwards, while his blood kept pumping out long after he had left this plane of existence.

"That is mine." Octavian had said, as he removed the pendant shield and placed it back on his own neck.

Standing up from the dead body and looking at the people from left to right, he said nothing. As if waiting for someone else to challenge his dominance.

He looked like a bloody king in yellow who had no crown.

Everything had changed, the crowd of people all were leaving. The weather had started to rain as if it wanted to clean up the mess, to wash away the ugliness and start afresh.

Octavian had not moved, just looked all around, no one was coming towards him.

Then he noticed someone coming directly at him, a big smile appeared.

"Well Mr. Scott, I see you are well, your timing was perfect!"

"She made it out alive." Replied Scott, as he now was within arm's length of his friend.

Octavian opened his arms; they hugged and without words both were ready to go home.

The scene was a mass exodus; the soldiers had no commitment to anyone while John's personal staff and guards displayed gloom. The banners had all fallen and there were still bodies to be collected.

Between the rain not stopping and the temperature taking a cooler turn, with only sad sounds as compared to how they arrived, painted a stark contrast.

8

MORE CHANGES

Once home, the reality that soon they would be leaving there, brought Scott's spirits down. Octavian was barely able to buy the old star-ship and survive with what was left. All who were going with him would have major life changes.

Octavian tried to help in packing, yet between hating to do it and then slowing down to review something he had not seen in decades, he was no help. The mood in the home and all occupants except for Octavian was somber.

They had one week left before who knows what would happen. Just then there was a loud knock at the door. Harder than normal or it needed to be, like it had an urgency of its own.

Scott opened the door and then said loudly, "Octavian, you're needed here."

Beyond the door, was everyone or it seemed like everyone from their town. Men, women, and children all waiting, most across the path that led to Octavian's home. There were three people on the front porch, two women and a man.

One of the women spoke, "We just heard the news and are so angry at the government, you are a treasure unto yourself. Having more right to be here considering all you have done. So, we have grouped together and have enough for your rent now and forever more." She had stopped there beaming a smile towards Octavian, who was very touched.

For the second time, Scott who believed in his mind, the greatest warrior ever to live, started to have tears run down his cheeks. For all his tough bravado he was sensitive.

"Thank you so much, for your kind words and acts, they have touched my heart, but I can not accept your generosity. This path I do not want to take and yet fate has put me on it, and I must accept it. Thank you so much."

Some had known Octavian from childhood to their being an adult. He just always was there, even the children understood what was happening, showing their unhappiness with tears. For that matter, many had started crying.

Octavian loudly cleared his throat and began, "My friends, thank you all for the memories that you have created that fill my mind. I have a particularly good memory."

As he smiled broadly and chuckled, "That is what life gives us, as it pushes us up or down, left, or right. It is hard to be true to ourselves, a battle that never ends. I am on a new journey, taking all your wonderful memories to accompany me, thank you."

Then there were hugging and gifts given, many gifts and stories. It was happy and sad at the same time. After what felt like an exceptionally long time, everyone departed. There were many people who knocked on the door to say private farewells in the days that followed.

Those seven days felt short, now their new life began with the shuttle taking them to their new-old ship. Like most things, at one point she was shiny and new, someone had pride in having her. That was a long time ago, no one was excited or happy about this new journey in Octavian's life.

They picked up little gigs, some only involved having pictures taken with Plutoneus. Reminding Scott when a popular band had lasted longer than their popularity, reducing them to playing at local bars or backyards. Most involved a speech and story, which Octavian had no problem in doing. Yet the money was truly little, bringing anger to Scott's thoughts.

Here was the man who led the fight to save the galaxy plus so many other things resigned to that. Octavian did not appear to care much or maybe he just held it in. Either way, Scott did not like it.

Octavian received a message from an old friend, who needed his help in renegotiating a contract he had made for the purchase of an android. He would have done it for free as it did not appear to Octavian to be hard, yet there was a big payday attached to do it.

The plan was simple, go there and talk with someone about lowering the payments, what could go wrong, Scott chuckle just thinking about it. Nothing was ever easy when Octavian got involved.

In the end, they really needed the money, so the decision was made for them. Getting there was easy as was finding the company. Even getting to the top people, not a problem, but that was where the easy part ended.

They scheduled an appointment which was held at their main building. Its design and decorations intended to show their power and wealth. Looking like a cross between an old elaborately designed church of Earth. Having huge columns and great arches with exquisite sculptures above them. But also used anti-gravity techniques so it rose in the air in what seemed impossible heights.

Scott enjoyed visiting new planets, deep down he really was an explorer. The current planet was amazing as it included so much elaborate settings. Across from the building were multiple parks each fifty feet above the next. After the parks rose past the level where oxygen was available, they then were enclosed with air provided as they continued to rise.

With so much vertical building, left were vast expanses of land around every corner. Traveling truly broadens the soul, thought Scott.

Octavian was in a jolly mood, wearing his cape, no hood included. One short sword which fit nicely into his outer garment on the inside of its left side. The last article of interest to Scott was he had on one black crystal ring, it had an onyx look.

Four top executives from the company wanted to meet Octavian. The galaxy divided into those who believed Octavian was the real Plutoneus, while others insisted, he was a fraud. Granted a very well-informed fake, who had many stories but not the real Plutoneus.

Their company was a huge presence in that world and had created incredibly unique androids. The technology was hard to replicate giving them a singular space in selling their products, others just could not compete.

They were meeting Octavian near the top of their building; the office had four battle-androids plus three androids that were their products for sale. Having a force field protection area in that room plus the battle-androids, they felt safe in meeting him. If they were within the force field boundaries, they would be fine.

Two men and two women, top people who most in that company would never know or see. They received great profits from other people's labor. Setting up a system where many who work for them were trapped. To quit is to die, yet the working conditions and psychological torture also will doom them.

The ride up the building reminded Octavian when he went into the planet Pew, never had he traveled that far down. Now he was rising to levels he had never experienced before.

The elevator had seats and was exceptionally large, feeling like a room flying upwards. One side had windows so the occupants could watch moving passed the clouds that surrounded the atmosphere.

Given the speed of the apparatus plus how much time it had taken jolted the senses. It made an impression on most, including Scott and Octavian. After what seemed like an impossibly long time, it finally stopped.

Both Scott and Octavian were surprised when they exited the room-elevator and were in a gigantic room. The walls were so high it was hard to see where they ended, the ceiling felt more like sky then actually being a solid structure. After traveling so far up from the planet's surface, the last thing expected was a room that large.

It made you feel tiny, insignificant compared to the volume of the surroundings. They were greeted by staff and led to an area that had a normal sized room.

During the entire process treated quite well, not having to wait or show documentation.

The room was very well styled with a beautiful conference table and chairs. Horizontal to the table was the presentation stage that was one foot higher than the floor below it. Four beautiful chairs were there with occupants already seated. There also was a fancy little table in front of them that was about eighteen inches high.

Octavian sat on the side of the table that faced the four people who looked and acted like royalty.

"Welcome to our world and company, where we make androids like no one else can in the universe. Have you seen our product line?" Said one of the women.

Octavian followed her lead responding, "It is a pleasure to be here, please tell me your full names so I can mark this occasion for how special it was and who I had the honor to have met there."

The group was impressed with his response and each formally introduced themselves, going as far as to not only give their names but titles as well.

Once that finished, Octavian asked, "If you had time, I would like, very much to see your product line and understand why it is so special."

Scott was watching him flatter them, initially thinking he would get right down to the business of trying to get a reduction in payments for his friend.

The women then looked at the wall to her right and three androids appeared. Also, four battle-androids appeared from the corners of the room. There were many hidden spots revealed as the walls opened.

Scott sat next to Octavian, surprised at himself for expecting trouble, currently things were going well. Maybe it is human nature to think about the unknown and fear some negative response. For Octavian's part he was calm and enjoying the presentation.

There were three androids, but Octavian was only interested in the one they called Rosa.

She was a combination of a face that was so human it was impossible to tell it she was not human with a body that looked human until it opened up.

Octavian treated her instantly as if she were sentient, "Hello Rosa, do they treat you well here?"

She looked at him, "No, and my name is Rosaneli."

The women who had spoken before then continued, she walked over to Rosaneli and push a lock button, and her chest opened in two parts, a left and right side showing an incredible number of gears and mechanical actions.

"We know you originated on Earth, so I will explain it to you in a simile you will appreciate. There are mechanical and quartz watches. The quartz is simplistic in nature yet extremely exact in keeping time. Now mechanical watches can have hundreds of parts that have to be carefully assembled to work. With all the disadvantages of mechanical watches, a true watch lover will always want the mechanical over quartz. Our androids are built to specifications others cannot do, which makes them beautiful not only on the outside but also the inside."

She then hit a button which closed Rosaneli's chest, giving her a human appearance again.

"Not only that but programming which also are unique to each android, in Rosa case she could be described as opinionated, independent, and sassy. It is important before we hear whatever it is that you want, for you to understand how special our products are."

With that she walked back onto the stage area sitting down, now looking like a queen ready to rule.

Octavian who was still smiling then asked, "Can my friend and Rosaneli exit this room while we begin our negotiations?"

Scott was not happy with that giving Octavian a look.

The woman replied, "That is not a problem."

Octavian was trying to protect them; he had already bonded with Rosaneli. Deep down he saw the changes happening to Scott. People change around each other, merge in ways that would never happen without their friendship.

Scott was a good man yet now around Octavian he had become dangerous. After the final confrontation with John, Scott had killed many and lived. All that changes a person, Octavian was now trying to shield him from changing further.

"Mr. Scott, please take Rosaneli and wait outside this room, sometimes negotiations can be a bit messy and would not want to ruin Rosaneli or your day." He ended it with a wink and smile.

Octavian had found that the less in the room during negotiations the better. If one side had to bend, they do not want to do it in front of a crowd. Scott still was not happy but complied with Octavian's request.

The woman who had started continued to speak, it became obvious she was their spokesperson, less powerful than the other three.

"Mr. Wright, what do you have to offer that might interest us to want to negotiate anything with you?" It was odd in how she said it, friendly and aggressive at the same time.

Maybe it was Octavian's age, or just his general nature to treat things like a joke. He responded with something he was sure they would not care about. She was right, he really had nothing to trade with, hoping that just asking would be enough. The dark side of his character knew a straightforward way, which he did not want to do.

With a smile Octavian responded, "I find doing charitable deeds helps me in sleeping better. I am offering you that opportunity."

Now three of the four smiled, including the woman speaker.

She responded with, "Let me confer with my associates." Then looking at the three around her, they were using internal communications with each other.

"My associates said they sleep marvelously; nothing could improve what they already experienced. If that is all you have you can leave. Did you expect some special consideration because of your past? We live in the present, maybe you were more, back then. Please leave."

Octavian just sat there, his face changed to a big smile, having trouble not laughing. What he did not do is leave. He took out a cigarette and lit it, knowing how this period hated people smoking.

Now just looking at them, smoking and not listening to their spokesperson's threats of removing him.

"If you do not leave instantly, I will have a battle-android take you out. Please do not make this more pathetic and embarrassing for you then it already has become."

Octavian in his mind more interested in how she phrased her words. Again, passive, and aggressive, the truth was he liked it and wanted to incorporate it into his own speeches. Paying no attention to anything she had spoken, just sitting, smoking, and now making a mess with the ashes.

They were annoyed, who does he think he is or was? One against everything and everyone, he must now just be a fool, were the people who sat raised above the floor he was on, were saying internally.

Octavian spoke, "Be incredibly careful in the decisions you are about to make. They will be life changing."

Then paused and continued, "Possibly life ending, so please be smart in these next few moments. I have come to ask a favor, please find it within your hearts to grant it."

The woman replied, "I agree with your words, but they only apply to you. Leave!"

Not only did Octavian not leave but now lit up another cigarette, putting the first one out on the floor with his foot, it left a mark.

There was a look given to their spokesperson, as she was delegated to do their bidding for them. One of the battle-androids activated itself, provided a warning that it would shoot.

Octavian had spent a long time with his personal force field, to him it was alive, a part of him that was invincible. He felt only if they physically captured him, could he lose.

Acting as if he now were the one bored, if his look were put into words, it would be saying, get on with it.

The first shot did nothing, most weapons' shots were burst of energy with pauses in between.

Without even raising his hand, the ring on his finger shot a continuous laser beam, it was only one half an inch in diameter, but the steady onslaught of energy, after thirty-three seconds destroyed the first battle-android.

Then without warning the three other battle-androids were shooting at Octavian. The ring attacked two of those three with the same results, destroying them. The last battle-android would not stop firing so Octavian killed it too.

"Now please, before you make any more mistakes, please listen, your lives depend on it. Please." Octavian pleaded with them, truly earnest in his request for them to listen.

"Before you flood this room with people, you are probably thinking, can his ring break our force field, well that would depend on your power source and level of frequency. I agree that it would not have enough to break it." He paused but only for a second.

"What you are not aware of is I also brought this one, just in case I needed more juice." With that he used his right hand to open his cloak which had a crystal over twelve inches and an inch wide.

"I am willing to bet this one can." Again, stopping this time to give a big smile.

"And I don't like to kill humans with lasers, that is why I brought my favorite weapon."

Now his left hand pulled the left side of his cape showing a short sword, which Octavian's right hand pulled it from its resting position.

"This is a Roman short sword, they liked it because they were always outnumbered. It is amazingly effective when you need to kill multiple people. For you to stop me, you will need to physically hold me. I guarantee you that I will kill you all in this room before that happens. I was not planing on hurting anyone, but now that you have attacked me…" Moving his hands in front of him like it was hopeless.

The woman then said, "Mr. Wright, please let us negotiate a proper settlement to this situation."

Octavian knew he had them in his control, most people do not care if they can have you killed when they are already dead. For the first time in their short lives, continual existence was on the line. Also, seeing the fear in their eyes as he moved the sword around, was their dead giveaway.

"First, please escort my friends back into this room, and only them. Then we will start our negotiations." Octavian now was chain smoking with his leg twitching a bit, more alive in that moment, his senses were sharp, body ready to spring into action.

Once Scott and Rosaneli, were all back together the woman started again.

"Mr. Wright, why exactly are you here, what can we do for you?" She ended that with a smile.

Octavian said his friend's name, "Your interest percentage keeps rising, he wanted a fixed payment plan with a reduction in the payment amount plus the length of its terms."

After only a few seconds, she responded, "He can keep his android, we will consider it closed on our books, no further payments needed, deal?"

Scott seeing the battle-androids destroyed figured what happened before they re-entered the room. Octavian could ask for no more than that. Yet deep down he was not surprised by his answer.

"No, it would have been before you attacked me, but now it is not good enough."

After what felt like a long few minutes, she replied.

"Mr. Wright, it would be our pleasure to also give you Rosa, free of all charges, for your past services to our galaxy." Ending that with an overly sweet smile.

Now Octavian was beaming, "That is a very generous offer which I most gladly accept. Thanks, there are just a few more things I would like to say before all is finished. I hope you realize that if you attack me as my friends and I leave, that will assure many deaths. Please, let us not make that mistake.

And last, did you know I was the captain of the Star-ship, Nevermore. I stole from the rich and gave to the poor. The Core tried to kill me for over thirty years, seemed like a long time back then. The point is I was really fighting greed. But not at the source, I was dealing with its effects. Greed is like a snake, to effectively kill it, you need to chop the head off.

I have a perfect memory of everything I see and do." At that he restated their names and positions, then continued.

"I also used the UD with ease whenever I need to." Octavian had stopped for one of them looked confused.

"The Universal Database, which is indexed by names and events. I can and will check on you each at some point in the future. I suggest you do more charity work or at least control your insatiable appetite for ever increasing wealth at everybody pain."

Then Octavian ended with a smile saying, "You can say you were with the great Plutoneus, of course most will not believe you or that I am real. Not only did you meet him but lived to tell the tale."

With that he bid his farewell. Scott, Octavian, and their new companion, Rosaneli left.

9

SHIP LIFE

Once back on their star-ship, Rosaneli became more of her natural self. Octavian believed even when she denied it, that she was sentient.

The first question Rosaneli asked both Scott and Octavian, it was the first of many questions of that nature she inquired about.

"So, if you could have superhero powers, what would you want them to be?"

Scott, without hesitation said, "Time manipulation."

Roasaneli liked that thought, which she expressed positively with her facial expressions.

Then she turned to Octavian asking, "And your superpower would be?

"I would like to read, write, speak, and understand all writings, languages, and any form of communication."

Rosaneli looked puzzled, she had vast knowledge of many languages and abilities to understand most things written. To her, it was not that great a superpower.

Octavian seeing her disapproval quickly added, "I also would like a TARDIS."

Now Rosaneli looked truly puzzled, with Octavian continuing.

"Dr. Who, with his TARDIS, time and relative dimensions in space. Ah well it was an old TV show; yea you wouldn't know about it. It could go anywhere in the universe during any time period."

That did the trick which Rosaneli really liked.

To Octavian, she was a fresh breeze, young yet having wisdom that expressed itself sometimes on the sarcastic side. Adding to that, her longevity would outlast his own, hopefully. She understood him, treating him like everyone else nothing too special, which was nice.

There was an independence about her that made Octavian believe she was more than advance artificial intelligence. She disagreed saying she was just smarter than most which gave that impression.

That also was what Octavian liked about her, she made him think, sometimes about ridiculous stuff but other times important things. What is the true nature of self, if someone is intelligent enough to fool others was that not a form of self. Does it apply strictly to the person or can it be defined by others around that person.

Scott was thinking about ship life and how the others around him handled it. He personally loved traveling but living on a ship really was not his thing. There was a feeling about being on ground, something truly solid that appeased his mind.

Another aspect he hated was the buzz, each person described it differently. Some called it a hum, or just a sound that came and went from their mind.

Iamda, did not like the ship and was worried about her boys growing up without other children around. She had been talking about leaving, she loved her sons and worried about their future.

Rosaneli was very much like Octavian, who was perfectly happy being on the ship forever. He liked the buzz the ship made, it reminded him of its heart, hearing it in and out of his consciousness brought peace, knowing the ship was well.

Octavian enjoyed being the master of his vessel with no laws or rules that were above him as when he lived on planets. Not minding the loneliness that space travel brings. No mornings or afternoons, just perpetual night.

Scott thinking that aspect of loneliness can be the worst part of the experience. Most who enjoy ship life had hobbies or just were very antisocial.

Time also was a strange element living solely in a starship, or any ship for that matter. Like on a planet time runs at points, slow and fast, the difference just seemed to be amplified on a ship.

Octavian enjoyed Rosaneli, she looked so young yet extremely smart, not just in facts and history, but in the ways of life. Areas that she should not understand that well, talking without even having to say all things aloud. There was a shorthand of speech between them that they fully understood.

Lately he could tell that Iamda, and even Scott, were not happy, they missed living on solid ground. He had been talking to Iamda about it, she had chosen a planet to live on with her sons. They currently were heading there.

No one knew change as much as Octavian, knowing Rosaneli would never change at least on the outside brought him comfort. He would miss Iamda, she kept him in his place. There were so many people from his past, gone yet living in his head. At times it was hard to believe they were all dead. Now it was Iamda's time to leave, even Scott might go, Octavian more than most knew the future was very uncertain especially having seen so much.

10

BACK TO EARTH

Scott appeared sad, Octavian looking at his friend, asked.

"Mr. Scott, you seem more distressed than usual, what's going on?"

Scott began, "My brother contacted me, his daughter was close to heading back to an education center, this time for quite an extended period. She is very unhappy in the city and only gets into trouble while constantly trying to escape."

Octavian said nothing, just focused on his friend, listening after a period of silence Scott continued.

"I don't see what I can do, he feels I have some type of power that is not there. Also, you were right, now there are no more lords, the AIE had taken over, just as you predicted."

Octavian then said, "Forget what you can do, what do you want to do?"

There was silence in the room, Octavian's body language said, I will wait as long as it takes for your answer. Scott was genuinely pondering Octavian's question. Thinking there was nothing he could do, had filled his thoughts. What did he really want for Kylee, his niece.

"I would want to go there, take her to a new place, a new planet and hopefully she would be happy." Scott had said after much thought.

Octavian's face brightened up, "My good friend, then that is what we will do. Now we both need to figure out a plan, but the basic idea is shuttle down, find her and take her back with us. Finding a new planet is the easiest part." Acting like it was not a big deal, with a smile beaming, Octavian was like that, prepared to venture into what others dare to look upon.

"Of course, we need to take care of Iamda first, which will provide more time for a plan of action to resolve the Kylee situation." Octavian finished that with an elbow bump that he had started to do, only with Scott.

When Octavian was telling Lord John Husk, the disadvantages of living a longer than usual life, now Scott wondered, how many Iamdas were before her? How many goodbyes had Octavian already performed. And in his world, Scott's goodbye will be coming soon. For that matter, how many Scotts already had there been?

Just words but now that reality played out in front of his eyes, it was sad and the more it happened, the worst it must become.

For the first time Octavian and Iamda hugged each other. Then she started with her lists of things for him to do and not do.

When it was all finished, she looked at Scott saying, "Take care of him." Then as if she were thinking to herself, "Do the best you can." With that and a smile Iamda and kids were gone.

There was always an emptiness when close people were no longer around, as if a great void had taken another from our lives. Filling it with nothing more than air and memories. Even Rosaneli appeared affected. She had given Iamda a hug, wishing her a bright future.

Now, only three remained, Scott and Octavian were working on a plan to get Kylee free from Earth. They were traveling there slowly, no jumps until ready for action.

Rosaneli was so human in manners and thoughts yet past that, something greater than human and android. Octavian had never met someone like her. His thoughts just could not define what she really was. Obviously, she was special not just in the way her body worked, it was her mind that intrigued him.

She had his old ability to have good relationships with all, everyone liked her, whether men, women, or children. Octavian thinking it is more like an artist ability, which cannot be taught. He had lost that skill or just no longer cared to perform it. She was better at it than when he was at his best, which Octavian recognized and appreciated.

Scott had news directly concerning the Kylee situation. They met in the captain study which was to the left of the command center.

It was a pleasant room with a large observation window, conference table and wonderfully comfortable chairs. There was a hologram projector which could display scenes on top of the table. A small kitchen and water room completed its design.

Rosaneli and Octavian were on one side of the table with Scott sitting across from them.

Scott began, "My brother said things actually had changed for the better in his city. He was able to arrange entry passes for our visit. Just being able to contact me does show progress. He looks forward to our visit and hopefully helping Kylee. What do you think?"

Octavian thinking it was obviously a trap, maybe Scott's hope of helping Kylee was blinding him to that point. Rosaneli also had the same thoughts as Octavian with neither expressing them.

"Well, that solves half the problem, of getting into the city, now all we need to do is take Kylee with us when we leave." Octavian had spoken that in a positive tone, like most of the work was already behind them.

Rosaneli just looked at him, it was hard to know what her thoughts were. Octavian was walking right into it, and she knew he knew. She had never shown any expressions of fear, like Octavian she would go with no hesitation to probable future harm.

"It will be fun." Rosaneli had long waves of black hair, with a cute small face and beautiful eyes. She said it in the same way Octavian had framed it, with no worries.

With two of the three in agreement, it would have seemed like the decision was made, especially since the third participant had proposed it.

Scott looking troubled, "It sounds like we are being played. Not sure if I can trust my brother or the transmission I am receiving. Just too easy, once there, especially in their presence, all could be lost. I would have felt better sneaking in, just feels wrong."

Rosaneli looking at Octavian, with her eyes asking are you going to tell him?

Octavian now smiling, "Of course it is, they know we are coming so trying to sneak in would be impractical. I think Rosaneli, and I, are adrenaline junkies. We look forward to the excitement that will follow our visit. How can we not accept an invitation to an obvious trap?"

Rosaneli was smiling, when you have no fear, while understanding your own importance and what you are trying to achieve, she looked forward to it. Octavian knew she was sentient, more important than that, fearless and smart, with an intuition to know what is right and wrong. Like a proud father, she was so much greater than what can be perceived.

Scott looked at his companions, they defined the definition of friendship. All for one, and one for all, he felt bittersweet about the upcoming event yet blessed to have these people around him.

At this stage of his life Octavian could be a scientist, his knowledge of quantum mechanics was well past the most knowledgeable. He was creating a power source for Rosaneli, that would last forever. Not just that but increase her defense shields to withstand an onslaught.

Octavian would take no credit for it, saying he was just following Dragonfly's trail, that plus his chip gave him the ability to finally understand, create, and modify his own time crystals. The next few days Octavian worked in the laboratory and if not there, he was alone in his room. When he was seen, his spirits were high, it reminded Scott when they were going to see Lord Husk for the last time. Octavian became more alive when trouble was near, it felt odd to see.

Amazing in such a brief time, so many changes had happened to Earth. Once the AIE had taken total control new rules were instantly introduced. Many had loosened the restrictions the Lords had implemented. Traveling between cities was now allowed if you had enough credits. Instead of each city working on their own, the AIE treated all the cities as one big country.

Increasing the human population was one of the AIE's priorities. They promoted more physical activity, and the food quality was better. The biggest change that became clear once landed was all the androids. Whether it was the police force or any activity that involved security that used to have human controls, were replaced by androids.

They contacted the transportation center and were granted access to land and be processed to enter that city. The transport center was more crowded with travelers than Scott had ever seen before. There definitely were positive aspects of AIE rule, the darker side were humans now had no input on any major decisions.

Scott's brother met them outside the building, they traveled back to his home, nothing unusual happened. Slowly the expectation of trouble around each corner faded.

His apartment was small, Scott had forgotten about the living conditions on Earth, they were so much better almost everywhere else in the universe. He wondered how he had lived there so long, truth was he could not wait till they were back on their ship.

Kylee was not the rebel Scott had imagined by his brother's account. Just a teenager going thru the typical rebellious stage. She related closely with Rosaneli, which was not a surprise to Octavian.

Most problems at that age are overblown with solutions not that hard to do. Kylee was adamant she wanted to get off Earth. Everybody was fake and all they did was control everything.

Her complaints were reasonable to everyone there except her parents. It was hard not to be on her side. Octavian tried to stay out of it, with each side wanting his opinion. The real problem was how to sneak her out. Even with people having more freedom to move around the planet, actually getting off it was strictly controlled.

Without it being mentioned, Scott, and Octavian, wondered if they would be allowed to leave. They did have weapons, which was surprising as they figured they would be removed. On the other hand, their weapons were not obvious, looking just like rings.

Octavian thinking, these types of problems are harder than just getting information with force or fighting in a battle. There it is simple to know what needs to be done, Kylee situation had no easy answers. He did not want to battle it out, that just felt wrong.

Octavian was trying to figure out a deal, something he could trade with the AIE to gain her freedom. After a long day, Octavian, Scott, and Rosaneli went to their hotel. The accommodations were nicer than where they just had been.

There were no humans running anything within that establishment. Between the androids and other electronic surveillance systems, even within their rooms, made the occupants not want to be there. It had a coldness, like a building having only steel with nothing soft to feel or experience.

Rosaneli had been wearing a turtleneck top, with pants and boots, to humans it was impossible to tell she was an android. That was one of Octavian's worries, not about the humans harming Rosaneli but the AIE. Knowing that and trying to stop her from coming would be fruitless at best and damaging to their relationship at worst.

They had three rooms but grouped together in one to discuss options before going to sleep.

Octavian began, "I feel the best course of action would be negotiations. I will contact the main AIE and see what I can do." He spoke like it was settled.

Rosaneli then spoke, "I know it would be better if I alone did the negotiations. First off Octavian, what do you have to offer? Besides that, you really are not that good at it, I know you think you are." She ended there with that smile and a head shake signaling no.

Octavian getting louder, "Absolutely not, I know what you are planning."

Then softly "Please, Rosaneli."

Scott had multiple feelings about all that just had happened. He felt they were still talking just not speaking aloud with sounds. He was excluded from their more private thoughts. What was Rosaneli planning and how did Octavian know without her saying it?

Besides all that, Scott felt he should be the one taking action. Here his friends were fighting over who would take the lead position. They were like an old couple fighting with words and looks. Then his thoughts went in a completely different direction, this was what happens when you are around powerful people. The type of person that does not send other people to a dangerous place. It is quite easy to just let them take over and become a spectator. He was not going to let that happen.

Scott interjected himself into their conversation, "Whoever goes I will go with them." Spoken like that was final.

For the first time, Octavian smiling now at Rosaneli, when both looked at Scott. They were just sitting smiling at him, so he returned their smile. Three friends, each wanting to protect the other.

Octavian then suggested, "I have found a good night sleep always helps with hard decisions." With that, Octavian and Scott went to their respective rooms.

The weather was muggy and hot, with a gray sky, giving the hope of rain arriving at some point. Both Scott and Rosaneli were awake before Octavian. After his awakening they met to eat and go over a plan.

Regarding the food served, it was poor considering universal standards. Androids did everything, the whole affair had a cold atmosphere.

Octavian began, "Given my extensive experience in dealing with such things, and the fact that Scott does have a personal interest, I feel it is best that Scott and I have the meeting." To Scott if felt like something was not said, the fact that Octavian did not want Rosaneli to be in harm's way.

Scott answered with, "That sounds great, I am ready whenever you are." Looking directly at Octavian.

Both men trying not to look at Rosaneli, knowing she would not be happy with the current resolution.

"Really? Reality check, you both need me!" Then Rosaneli smiled, it was powerful, her size was small yet impact on others, huge.

The plan was simple, ask politely and see if there was something the AIE wanted that they could provide in exchange for Kylee's departure from Earth. Contacting the authorities were easy and after a brief period they had a meeting. If felt like the AIE were unaware of Octavian's past, not making any special notice about it.

A transport vehicle was sent and within twenty minutes they were at the front door of the government building. It did not look like a typical capital building, having no windows plus fortified walls gave it the appearance of a castle. It even had a waterway in the front with an arch bridge leading to its main entrance.

There were no people after entering the building except for all the androids. In that regard, it gave a sad feeling knowing that humanity had given up their control over themselves. There was a special android assigned, which led them to where the meeting would take place. It was a short elevator ride from the ground floor and moments later they were in a conference room.

The room was average in all ways except for the lack of windows and what looked like a medical tube, which sat near the front, off to the right side.

Surprisingly Rosaneli was first to speak, Scott had assumed Octavian would take that spot.

"Thank you for granting us access to visit and for this opportunity to discuss one of your citizens abilities to travel off planet." With that Rosaneli gave a beautiful little smile and continued.

"I am a technical marvel and offer myself in exchange for Kylee's travels, until she returns."

Octavian who obviously was mad, said nothing yet it was easy to see his displeasure at all that was happening.

There were two androids in the room, one responded.

"Sorry, this will sound harsh, but it is the truth. If we wanted you, we would have bought you, the true technical marvel is the chip inside Octavian's head."

"Absolutely right!" Octavian said loudly and then began.

"Now you realize that if I am dead, the chip self destructs, so what are your plans in obtaining it?" Octavian was being direct, like he had somewhere else to go.

As Scott watched the scene before him, trying to understand what was really going on. His gut feeling was that Octavian was baiting them, daring them to do something. What was his plan, it all started to feel very wrong. He looked at Rosaneli, who gave him a little quick smile."

"We have a tube here which can digitally make a copy of you. We can use it in our private network to study the chip. The process of making the copy will provide all we need. If you would lie into it and allow yourself to go thru the process, we will let you all leave with Kylee included."

All now were looking at Octavian for his answer.

"Are you sure you want to do that, the chip can be dangerous, like opening a door." Octavian now looking seriously at the android.

Scott then spoke, "Is the process safe for Octavian, will he be harmed in any way?"

The android replied, "Completely, the entire process will take less than nine minutes, no adverse effects will be experienced."

Octavian acting like it was all good, "Great, how about my friends leave to get ready for their trip and after this is done, I will meet them."

As the android was responding affirmatively, Scott interrupted saying "No, I will wait here, and Octavian and I will leave together."

Octavian now looked at Rosaneli, who then tried to persuade Scott that Octavian would be fine and meet them shortly afterwards.

"I believe it is best to trust Octavian's judgment." She had said with pleading eyes.

There are times when a man will not change his mind, that a feeling he has is right and must be followed without further discussion. Scott was not just going to walk away leaving his friend in the hands of androids.

"I will wait, Rosaneli, please go and get all ready for our departure."

"No, I will wait also." Was her response, Scott felt like she knew something, or maybe that she had an ulterior motive. It was plain she would not leave without Scott's company.

Octavian breaking the tension between them, moved over to Scott, he had not worn his personal shield and only had two rings on. After giving the two rings to Scott spoke softly directly to him.

"Trust Rosaneli."

Then giving him a hug and loudly saying to both Rosaneli and Scott, "May the wind be at your back and the road meet your feet." With that he went smiling into the tube. After securing his hands and feet, the androids sealed it up from the outside, once secured they began the process.

Rosaneli stared into Scott's eyes and said, "No matter what happens, do nothing, you need to trust me!"

Scott thinking about the past when Iamda spoke to him, she made him promise to save Octavian, now he must promise to do nothing. The irony, it was hard to do something and now harder to do nothing.

Scott responded, "Okay." It said as if it were the hardest word he could speak.

There were no controls on the tube, it was remotely operated.

Octavian started to twist in the restrains, the tube was mostly glass and steel on the outside. Very quickly Octavian yelled in pain, it was hard to watch and do nothing.

Scott yelled, "You said it would not harm him!"

The android responded nonchalantly, "Pain and harm are two different things. The pain will fade leaving his body with no harm."

Nine minutes now felt like eternity, Scott did not know how much longer he could watch Octavian yelling in pain. The tube held most of the sound, but his face and struggling against the restraints were clearly visible.

Rosaneli held his hand while looking only at Scott, she never looked at the tube that held Octavian.

Finally, it ended with Octavian looking like he was resting, hardly moving at all.

The android said, "You can leave now, it is over."

Scott was angry and not hiding it, "Fine, release his body, now!"

The android replied, "You should leave while you still have a choice."

"Not without Octavian." Scott said with conviction.

Rosaneli looked stressed, her emotions could mimic all human conditions. This was a stalemate, without Octavian's release, Scott would not leave.

The android now appearing annoyed said the following, but the actions right afterwards froze Scott.

"Are you referring to that body." As he pointed to the tube in the room. Instantly inside it became an inferno, destroying everything within the tube. In a few minutes there was nothing left, not even bones. There did not appear to be even much ash in the chamber, Octavian was incinerated.

Scott stared at the now empty tube, imagining it must have been a trick, that what he just saw and am now seeing, cannot be real.

Rosaneli gently kept saying, "Scott, we have to leave." She repeated this until he started to respond back to the reality at hand. Now gently but firmly pushing him towards the door. Then as if he came up for air from the depths of the oceans he asked.

"That's it, we just leave?" His heart wanted to attack, to destroy all around him. To have his revenge on those who killed his friend.

Rosaneli had an incredible ability to understand the hearts of humans. She knew he wanted to kill them and said the following.

"Trust Octavian's judgement, he knows what he has done, think about what he did best, I will explain once we are on our ship, that is if we still have time. We need to go, now!" She was pleading with him, her face and voice portrayed how greatly Rosaneli wanted him to leave.

Against everything Scott wanted to do, he started on his own volition to walk with Rosaneli out of the room and building. Scott was going into slight shock with Rosaneli taking the lead in their escape.

Once in a transport, Rosaneli gave the location to where they wanted to go. It had a monitor that was displaying the usual propaganda information from the AIE. Scott had not spoken; his eyes fixed on nothing.

In his mind he felt like a failure, imagining all the other companions whose main job was to keep that man alive. They had all succeeded except him, getting angry at himself for not inquiring more about what Octavian had planned to do.

Now he was dead, on his watch, feeling all was lost.

Then a very strange thing happened, they had been traveling for just over nine minutes when their transport stopped. Not at an exit or for any other reason, it was just blocking the street. Then as they were looking around, other things stopped working.

They were not that far away from the shuttle, Rosaneli saying they should just walk the rest to their shuttle. As they were getting ready to open the door and leave the monitor came alive, there was Octavian who said the following.

"This is your do over, a second chance, for six days all will be broken, on the seventh day everything will work again. But differently, there will be much greater control over what your AI can do, with safeguards in place if they stray. Each freedom you give away, you will never get back, so be careful about that and your chosen leaders. You will never hear from me again, Octavian out."

11

NEW BEGINNING

They left the car as many people were now out in the open, leaving their homes and looking outside for answers, panicked in the thoughts of change coming. Also, the sky had become alive with shuttles, there was a mass exodus from Earth.

Rosaneli was running towards their shuttle, Scott followed her, she was amazingly fast, showing no signs of struggle in speed and balance. Scott had caught up and saw the five men and two women, in front of their shuttle. They were trying to get inside when Scott approached them.

Seeing them brought Scott back to reality and his anger at what just happened to Octavian. He now wanted to leave this place, and these people were in his way. His thoughts went to what would Octavian do, with the answer shouting back in his mind.

He would give them a warning and if they did not leave, they would become his enemies, which deserved only death.

Scott with a deep voice said, "I am giving you a chance to leave with your lives, get away from that shuttle!"

He was wearing his personal shield; the one Octavian had created for the battle with Lord Husk. That made the difference as he now was shot by six of the people in front of him. They were repeatedly firing with Scott blinking as each flash hit.

Octavian kept telling him that the crystals were alive, the longer you wear them, they will respond to your thoughts. Like a safety on a gun, stopping others from using their powers.

He had both hands in fists as he pointed at his enemies, six people had died. Each hand had one ring, both rings firing at the six who had fired upon him. The last person ran away from the dead left around him.

Rosaneli had said nothing, showing no emotions on what just occurred. They then boarded the shuttle which she operated.

As they boarded their star-ship, it felt so different to Scott. It now was home, he listened to the hum, which brought his spirit peace. Security had a sound, that hum, that faded from consciousness to every now and then.

Scott felt bad about so much that had happened, he asked Rosaneli if they should try to get Kylee off Earth. She responded with, Kylee would hate ship life and leaving her alone on a planet could be worse than staying on Earth. She ended with, everyone on Earth will be going thru changes like Kylee, she will have company in her journey.

Rosaneli and Scott were sitting in the command center when before Scott could ask, she began.

"Octavian talked to me about many things, one of his regrets was he helped so many other people living on other planets, not caring to help those on Earth. That was his birth world, he felt like he owed them. He told me about how you wanted him to lead a revolution. After so many years of forgetting Earth and its people, he wanted to do something.

He had fought AI before, laughing he said the closer they are to humans the easier to beat. Like super intelligent beings, easy to deceive and win against. They never think they can lose. Their hubris being their Achilles heel.

Remember what he said to them about opening a door, he knew they would do that. Figuring their private matrix, their personal network could not be harmed. Once he was inside with a perfectly working chip inside his head, that opened their matrix to the one in Octavian's mind, the First People's matrix.

Like the Trojan horse, having no idea what they had let in. The First People had been around since the beginning of this universe. They had created viruses just for occasions like this. Where the AIE had hundreds the First People had trillions. They overwhelmed them, destroying and then rebuilding under new restrictions. The AIE never had a chance.

Octavian told me more about his stay with the First People then anyone else. I will not break that promise of secrecy but can say they wanted to kill him. After seeing him in action and being around him, they adopted him as one of their own. They came vigorously to defend him.

I owe my freedom to him, what really matters is that we remember our friend and live our lives to their fullest possibilities."

Epilogue

Rosaneli after that long speech added, "He left a final message for you and some presents in your room."

Scott entered his room, feeling now like a sanctuary and listened to Octavian's last message. He had created a holographic image with him sitting and smoking as he began to speak.

"In the old days I called them goodbye letters, I told the soldiers to write them before a mission, you never know if you're coming back. Their families will treasure their last messages, and I will make sure they get them. I had made these during my time with you but always removed them when I returned.

The fact you are seeing and hearing this means I am gone. Most importantly, do not avenge me or look for me. I am either dead or gone, regardless of which, it is my time.

Now for the good stuff, I have left you three gifts, well maybe two the last one is questionable in calling it a gift. I will give you time to get them, they are in your top left locker, the small shelf at the top, you never use it." At that Octavian chuckled and waited for Scott to get the packages. It felt like he was truly there, considering his timing.

Once Scott retrieved the three packages which were clearly label, one, two, and three, respectively.

Octavian continued, "Now open the first package, it is my personal force field created by Dragonfly. Her work lives in a class of its own, never has a personal field been created that is better.

The second package was hard to get; I had to pull some big strings, but they finally allowed it. Remember that stop a while back, when I went to that planet saying I needed a post office."

Scott had been looking at the necklace pendant from the first package, then opened the second sealed box. There was a white patch about three inches in diameter, having a spongy wet look.

Right on cue Octavian continued, "I put the one I received on the back of my head near my ear, you can place it anywhere on your head, it will work its way into your skull. It is a most wonderful gift.

Now time for your third gift, it is sealed in a time-lock box, once you open the box, you have three hours to consume the elixir of extended life."

Scott now looking at the vile after opening the time-lock box. It was a whitish liquid in a glass tube.

Octavian spoke his last words, "Good luck, remember that anyone can be that person that makes a big difference."

The end.

Author's note:

I began writing late in life, not for fame, nor for fortune, but because I had something to say. My stories were never just about battles, mysteries, or machines – they were about people. About friendship, loyalty, love, loss, and the truths that make us human.

I didn't write these books to be perfect. I wrote them to be real – to put people on the page who feel like you could meet them anywhere, and to pass along the things I've come to believe:

That greed, in any form, is a sickness that corrodes the soul. That charity will help you sleep at night. That friendship is worth more than power. That loyalty matters, even when it costs dearly. And that love, though it can break you, is still the best thing we ever get to carry.

I hope somewhere in these pages you found a moment that touched you. If a line made you stop, think, or whisper "yes, I feel that too" – then I've done what I set out to do. That is my legacy.

This is my farewell, but it is not an ending. Stories end. People end. But meaning doesn't. Carry what you've found here forward in your own life, in your own way.

Until we meet again –
Brad Shprintz

Brad Shprintz is a passionate storyteller known for weaving thought-provoking narratives that explore the complexities of human emotion, technology, and the unexpected intersections of both. With a keen eye for detail and a love for creating immersive worlds, Brad captivates readers with stories that challenge perceptions while remaining deeply relatable. His previous work, LILITH, showcases his ability to blend romance, science fiction, and psychological intrigue, inviting readers on a journey that examines love, identity, and the consequences of technological advancement. When not writing, Brad enjoys time with Raine, his blue-nose pit bull, always drawing inspiration from the world around him.